A sure bet . . .

"C'mon, Lilly, just one more dance. That bet—it's about having a date. A real date," Charlie said nervously.

"Oh, I get it. We're supposed to look like we're on a date. Here, maybe this will help." Lilly put her hands on Charlie's shoulders and gazed up into his eyes. It was the least she could do after he'd fixed her father's car so well.

Charlie looked shocked as he put his hands on her waist. They moved slowly around the dance floor, swaying to the romantic music. Charlie pulled her a little closer as they squeezed past another couple.

Lilly didn't push him away. She looked up at him, and saw him smile. She was getting carried away with the sexy music and suddenly felt an irresistible urge to kiss him.

The song ended, and Lilly just stood there, her arms around Charlie. She was enjoying the moment, wishing this were a real date, that Charlie wasn't using her to win a stupid bet. Until she remembered how obnoxious, rude, and strange Charlie Roark usually was.

Boy, this wedding stuff is really getting to me, Lilly thought to herself. *I can't believe I almost kissed Charlie Roark!*

Don't miss any of the books in *Love Stories*
—the romantic series from Bantam Books!

Love Stories

The Day I Met Him

CATHERINE CLARK

BANTAM BOOKS
NEW YORK · TORONTO · LONDON · SYDNEY · AUCKLAND

RL 6, age 12 and up

THE DAY I MET HIM

A Bantam Book / August 1995

Produced by Daniel Weiss Associates, Inc.
33 West 17th Street
New York, NY 10011

ISBN: 0-553-56664-4

Published simultaneously in the United States and Canada

Bantam Books are published by Bantam Books, a division of Bantam
Doubleday Dell Publishing Group, Inc. Its trademark, consisting of the
words "Bantam Books" and the portrayal of a rooster, is Registered in
U.S. Patent and Trademark Office and in other countries. Marca
Registrada. Bantam Books, 1540 Broadway, New York, New York 10036.

PRINTED IN THE UNITED STATES OF AMERICA

OPM   0 9 8 7 6 5 4 3

Chapter One

"I'M TELLING YOU, Tracy, everything in my closet is ancient." Lilly Cameron stared at the collection of clothes in her closet, twirling the bright red phone cord around her wrist. "And there's no way I'm wearing that ugly paisley vest thing to Nicole's party tonight."

"Hey, it was just a suggestion," Lilly's best friend said. "You don't have to bite my head off."

Lilly laughed. "Sorry. I guess I'm a little wound up."

"It wouldn't have anything to do with trying to impress Bryan Bassani tonight, would it? Bryan I'm-new-here-and-I'm-too-good-for-Middleton-East-High Bassani?"

"You know if I were interested in Bryan, I'd be dating him already." Lilly inspected a sweater she'd worn practically all her sophomore year and tossed it to the back of the closet.

1

It was true—she'd never had a problem getting dates. Besides being outgoing and friendly, Lilly was pretty, with long dark brown hair and brown eyes. She was five feet eight inches tall, and she exercised at least five days a week—even in the dead of winter when she felt like drinking consecutive mugs of hot chocolate while lying on the couch.

"Admit it, Lilly. I know you like Bryan. You only spend all your free time talking about him," Tracy said.

"I do not," Lilly insisted. Could she help it if Bryan was the only guy at school who even remotely interested her at the moment? "I'm so sick of all my clothes!"

"Didn't you just spend a ton of money last weekend at the mall?" Tracy asked. "And didn't your mother tell you that was the absolute last pair of jeans you could buy until at least next year?"

"Oh, those." Lilly sighed. "I already wore them this week. Anyway, they're a really weird shade of green. I don't have anything that goes with them."

"Well, why don't you borrow something from your mom?" Tracy asked. "I bet you wear the same size clothes."

"Now there's a thought." Lilly's parents had gone away for the weekend to visit friends from college, and she had the house all to herself. She'd thought about throwing a party while they were away, but she knew she'd never get their permission.

Actually, her parents were pretty cool. Her father

had read some parenting book back when she was a baby, and he'd been referring to it ever since. Phrases like "Trust builds trust" and "Communication is caring with a capital *C*" had been drummed into Lilly's head all her life.

"I don't know about Mom's clothes," Lilly said. "But there is the most perfect sweater at the mall. The mannequin at the store modeled the sweater with my jeans. Oh, I just have to have it for tonight. Please take me to the mall, please, Tracy?"

"I can't," Tracy said. "I have to baby-sit my little brothers, and there's no way I'm taking *them* to the mall. Can you say 'total disaster'?" Tracy's brothers were nine and six years old, and Lilly knew from personal experience that they were impossible to keep track of. Once while baby-sitting they'd gotten separated at the park, and it had taken her and Tracy over an hour to find them.

"Then how am I going to get there?" Lilly said.

"I guess you could always walk," Tracy said. "It's only a couple of miles, right? Or you could ride your bike."

"Have you looked out the window today? It's pouring," Lilly said. "Rain-gushing-out-the-gutters pouring. I'd get drenched." It was early April in Maine, and that meant lots of rain—cold rain, the kind that cut right through to your bones.

"I guess you'll just have to find something else to wear," Tracy said. "You could always come over here and see if I have anything you want."

"Thanks, but no. I'll try to think of something

3

else," Lilly said. *Something boring,* she thought, *and old and tired-looking.*

"I'm still picking you up at eight, right?" Tracy asked. "That gives you at least three hours to find something fabulous to wear. Think you can manage?"

"Hey, stop making fun of me," Lilly said. "Is it my fault I want to look good?"

Tracy laughed. "Yeah, it is, now that you mention it. See you at eight."

Lilly hung up the phone and dropped onto the bed. The whole day was turning into an absolute waste. The parade Lilly and the rest of the cheerleading squad were supposed to march in had been canceled due to the rain and she'd been stuck inside all day, with nothing to do except watch TV, read, and listen to music. She couldn't go anywhere, unless she felt like swimming.

Maybe I should have tried to get a date for this afternoon, she thought. Actually, maybe she was better off without a guy. Lately her dates hadn't been much fun. First there'd been the guy who'd seen every *Star Trek* episode ever made—the old ones *and* the new spinoffs—and talked about them all night. Then had come the guy who thought a hot dog with Dijon mustard was fine dining. Not that Lilly had anything against hot dogs—at baseball games. But not when she was dressed for a fancy restaurant.

Her dates weren't always so bad, of course—some of them had been great. But for some reason they'd never turned into anything serious. And she was beginning to doubt whether she'd ever find her Mr.

Right. *Maybe Bryan Bassani's the one,* she thought dreamily. Not that she was going to impress him that night if she showed up in a lame outfit. She just had to find a way to get to the mall.

Getting her driver's license a few months earlier hadn't changed her life very much so far. Her parents rarely let her borrow one of their cars. To be fair, it was because they worked at opposite ends of town and it wouldn't make sense for them to drive together.

But then there were the weekends. Like that weekend, for instance. They were in New Jersey while she was stuck at home all alone, lying on her bed, trying to see pictures in the swirls of the textured ceiling above.

There *was* a car in the garage, though. Lilly just wasn't allowed to drive it. Sweetpea—her father's prized 1968 Volkswagen Bug. The one he'd had since college. The one he waxed every other weekend. The one he'd written poems about.

Her father had taught her to drive in the Bug, sitting beside her and coaching her on the smoothest way to downshift from third to second, but since then he'd been pretty stingy about letting her use it by herself. She could understand why—it *was* a great car. Although Lilly thought her father was insane to be so in love with a car.

No, he'd never let her drive it. But he didn't have to find out she'd used it, did he? She'd have the car back in half an hour. Lilly picked up her jacket and ran downstairs.

But as she grabbed the keys off the hook on the refrigerator, the phone rang. "Hello?" she said breathlessly.

"Lilly, hi!" Mrs. Cameron's voice cheerfully greeted her.

"Oh, um, hi, Mom!" Lilly replied. "What's up?" She felt a nervous flutter in her stomach. *You've got lousy timing, Mom,* she wanted to say.

"Just calling to make sure everything's okay. We're having a wonderful time here and we're sorry you didn't come. How's everything there?" Mrs. Cameron asked.

"Fine, Mom." Other than the fact she was about to use Sweetpea without their permission, everything *was* fine. "The weather's lousy, so the parade was canceled, but other than that, everything's great," she said. "Really, really great."

"Good, I'm glad to hear that. Well, we're heading out to a movie, so I'd better not chat for long," Mrs. Cameron said. "We'll be home late tomorrow night—take care of yourself, okay?"

"I will. Have fun! And have a safe drive home," Lilly said.

"We will. Good-bye!"

"Bye." Lilly hung up the phone and studied the car keys in her hand. She couldn't help feeling that her mother's phone call was some sort of omen. It was almost as if her conscience were speaking to her, telling her not to use the car, that her parents were watching and knew her every move.

"I've been watching way too many old *Twilight*

Zone episodes," she said out loud as she opened the door to the garage. She pressed the button of the automatic door opener and the garage door opened, dripping water all over the dry concrete floor inside. It was raining pretty hard—she'd have to be careful driving.

Lilly got into the Bug, closed the door, and slipped the seatbelt around her. She was glad she and her father were the same height—she didn't have to adjust the mirrors at all. That meant she didn't have to worry about returning them to the exact position he used.

She knew she shouldn't be doing this. If her father found out, she'd be in major trouble. But he would never know. The store was only two miles away, and he'd hardly remember whether the odometer reading was 89,842 or 89,846.

"Freedom!" Lilly screamed as she turned the key in the ignition.

Tapping her fingers on the black steering wheel to the beat of her favorite song blasting from the car stereo, Lilly couldn't have been any happier. She was even taking the long route home from the mall, down a winding back road, because she didn't want the fun to end. It was still raining and she couldn't open the window and feel the fresh breeze on her face, but she was having a great time anyway. She had bought the sweater she'd wanted, and she knew she'd look great at the party that night. If only there weren't a small monsoon happening, the day would be perfect.

"When's Dad going to fix this stupid stereo?" Lilly muttered to herself. "I keep losing my station to static." Frustrated, she reached over to change the station, slowing down for a stop sign up ahead. *Easier said than done,* she thought, frowning. All the preprogrammed stations her dad had chosen were either classic rock, which she hated, or public radio, which was even worse.

Lilly glanced up at the road for a second, peering through the tiny windshield wipers that swished the water back and forth, making sure she was slowing enough for the intersection. Then she reached farther over to the dial on the right and glanced down at the small red stick that showed what station was tuned in.

"Dad really needs a digital tuner on this thing," she muttered. She wanted 104.1, but it didn't seem to be coming in. She flipped the dial in the opposite direction and tried 93.7. An oldies station blared the Monkees at her. She turned back to 104.1. She had to be close to getting something good.

She made a small adjustment to the right and—

Smack! Lilly's head jerked forward as the car came to a sudden stop. All she heard was the crunch of metal—a horrible, screechy, twisting noise. Then, looking up, she found herself face to face with a stop sign. She had stopped for the sign, all right. She had crashed right into it!

Chapter Two

LILLY SLOWLY GOT out of the car, rain streaming down her face and drenching her clothes. She wasn't hurt, but her legs were shaking so much she could hardly stand up on the muddy ground. Her heart was beating wildly as she stepped around to the front of the car, holding onto the wet signpost that was now bent where the car had made its impact. She closed her eyes for a second, afraid to see the damage.

When she opened her eyes, the first thing she saw was her father's custom license plate, SWT-P, now slightly dented. The front bumper was out of line, completely hanging off one end. The stop sign looked as if it were coming straight out of the car, like a tree growing out of a planter. Lilly stared at the front end of the car, unable to move, as the reality of what had just happened hit her.

She had crashed her father's favorite car—his Sweetpea, his most prized possession on this earth. There was now a signpost welded around the bumper, and there was no way to hide this from him.

"My life is over. Completely, totally over," Lilly said, pushing back the wet hair that was stuck to her forehead.

Lilly heard the sound of an approaching car and stepped onto the shoulder, trying to get out of its way. As it came closer she realized it was a tow truck and frantically waved her arms in the air. "Hey! Hey!" she yelled, jumping up and down.

The tow truck roared by, splashing through a large puddle and splattering Lilly with water and mud. "Aargh!" she screamed in total frustration. Things couldn't get any worse!

Charlie Roark couldn't believe it. He'd already towed six cars to Roark's Auto Body, where he worked, and the day was far from being over.

He was cruising down the road toward his next job, a jump-start, listening to one of his favorite Crosby, Stills, and Nash tapes, when he saw a familiar-looking girl with long brown hair jumping up and down by the side of the road. *Why is she waving so frantically?* he wondered. Couldn't she see the lights on top of the truck flashing? He was obviously on his way to—

"Wait a second," Charlie said, turning onto Blake Street. He'd spotted a green Volkswagen Bug next to a knocked-over stop sign. Wasn't that Lilly

10

Cameron . . . the most popular girl in school? He knew he should keep going, but she seemed to need some help.

I'll just go back for a second, make sure she's okay, he told himself, pulling into a deserted parking lot to turn around.

"Hey! Hey, Lilly! Do you need some help?"

Lilly looked over her shoulder. A red, slightly battered tow truck had pulled over by the VW Bug, and a boy who looked vaguely familiar stepped out. His dirty-blond shoulder-length hair was in a ponytail under his faded green Roark's Auto Body cap. He walked toward her, wearing grease-covered jeans, a T-shirt, and tan work boots.

"Do I ever," she said, still wondering where she knew this guy from and how he knew her name. "Could you tow my car?"

"Well . . . sure," he said. "You're totally soaked. What happened?"

"Isn't it obvious?" Lilly replied. Then she smiled wanly. There was no point taking her frustrations out on this guy. Maybe, if she was nice, she could get Sweetpea fixed before her parents found out what she had done. "Hey, you go to Middleton East, don't you?" she asked as they walked back to Sweetpea. "You're in my English class—that's right! What's your name again? Stan? No, wait—it's Rick, isn't it?"

"Close," he said, looking irritated. "I'm Charlie Roark. Roark's Auto Body." He frowned and pointed to the cap. "I work part time for my dad and uncle."

"Right! Charlie. Charlie Roark. I guess I'm a little shaken up after what happened," Lilly said, trying to be friendly. This was going to work out even better than she'd hoped. Charlie just had to help . . . they were classmates, after all.

"So let's see what we've got here." Charlie took a walk around the car, and Lilly watched him carefully. He looked at her from the front of the VW and shrugged, a small smile lighting up his face. "This shouldn't be too hard to fix, but you never know."

"So, Charlie. Can I tell you something?" she asked. Lilly started to relax a bit as she looked into Charlie's eyes—his gorgeous blue eyes. He was good-looking, in a laid-back—extremely laid-back—kind of way. And she wondered why she'd never noticed him at school.

Charlie shrugged. "Sure."

"This is kind of embarrassing, but . . . I wasn't supposed to be driving this car. What I mean is, it's my father's car, and he's away for the weekend, and I . . . Let's just say I needed to get somewhere—it doesn't matter where—and . . ." She laughed nervously. "I guess I took my eyes off the road, and then, well, you can see what happened. The bottom line is, I'm not allowed to drive this car. And if my parents find out I did, I'll never drive again. And I'd just die if that happened." Lilly stopped to take a breath.

"So what are you driving at? No pun intended," Charlie said.

Lilly laughed, hoping that if she laughed at his jokes, she'd butter him up a little. "I need this fixed by tomorrow night," she said. "At the latest!"

"Yeah, right. Sure thing. As if that's possible," he said.

"What's the problem?" Lilly said. "Twenty-four hours is plenty of time. It's only a bashed bumper."

"First of all, there's no such thing as a little job when it comes to auto body," Charlie said, trying to pull the stop sign from the bumper. "And second, it's Saturday afternoon—closer to Saturday *night*. Past five. Our shop is closed from now until Monday morning, and there are at least six cars ahead of you from today alone. If you want us to fix it, you're looking at the end of the week, if you're lucky."

"What? The end of the week? That's impossible," Lilly said, shaking her head.

"No, that's how it is," Charlie said.

Lilly folded her arms over her chest and stared directly into his blue eyes. "Then I'll just have to call another shop," she said. "I'm sure someone can fix it by tomorrow. I'll just have to pay for overtime or something."

"You don't get it. Nobody works tomorrow. It's called a day off. Of course, since *you* don't work, you're probably not familiar with the concept."

"I do too work," Lilly said, interrupting him. "I've done tons of baby-sitting. And this summer I'll be waitressing at the country club."

"Yeah. Real tough. I rest my case," Charlie said.

"Look, waitressing *is* tough, for your information.

And you don't have to be so smug about everything," Lilly said. "I'm in serious trouble here. I need this car fixed before my father gets back tomorrow night. Will you help me or not?"

"Not," Charlie said with a shrug. "If you don't think we can do the work fast enough, then go ahead and call someone else. We don't need your little bang-up job here to survive, trust me."

"I'll just call another garage, then," Lilly fumed.

"Fine," Charlie said. "Good luck."

"You know, you're really insensitive. You don't even feel sorry for me," Lilly said, throwing up her hands.

"Hey, it's not my fault you don't know how to drive," Charlie replied.

"I do too!" Lilly practically shouted.

"Well, I'm sure that stop sign didn't jump out and hit you," Charlie said.

Lilly glared at him. "Brilliant, aren't you? You must be in *all* the honors classes."

"No, just trig and chemistry," Charlie said. "Have a nice weekend." He took a few steps backward.

"Are you just going to walk away without helping me? This is the biggest crisis of my life!" Lilly demanded.

"No, actually, I'm going to drive away," Charlie said calmly, walking toward the tow truck. "I have another car to help out. Have a nice day!" He got into the truck and slammed the door. A second later he took off, turning left at the intersection and heading down the road.

Lilly just stared at the truck, its flashing lights disappearing in the distance. How dare he strand her there! Didn't he have any sympathy? Did he have something against her, or what?

Suddenly Lilly had a vision. She saw herself at a student council meeting the previous fall, discussing the homecoming parade and their plans for floats. She'd been outlining the organization of the parade when somebody in the auditorium stood up and gave a speech about how wasteful parades were and how all those cars spewed too much carbon monoxide into the environment.

That had been Charlie Roark. And that had been the first and last time she'd noticed him . . . until now, of course. He'd made a big pitch for having the homecoming parade on foot or bicycle. And everyone had laughed, making jokes about the homecoming court riding down the street on handlebars, waving at people, or trudging all four miles in their high heels.

"Right! As if!" several people had shouted.

Charlie had left the room looking utterly defeated and humiliated. Lilly remembered she'd even felt a little sorry for him, because he'd looked so sincere, even if it was a stupid idea.

It served him right, she thought now. He deserved that and much more for what he'd just done to her!

She pulled off her wet jacket and tossed it in the back of the car. Then she crouched down in front of the car and tried to bend the bumper back into place. "Come on, Sweetpea," she coaxed, using all of her strength to pull at the bumper. "Come on."

Only it was a hopeless case. The patient wasn't going to come around. And thanks to Charlie Roark, Sweetpea was going to stay that way. Dead. Just like she would be, the second her parents found out what she had done.

Chapter Three

"FIXED BY TOMORROW. Right. And I'm going to be voted homecoming king next year," he muttered with a laugh. Lilly finding someone to fix that car in twenty-four hours was about as likely as Charlie running for the stupid student council. He could still remember how they'd treated him as if he'd just stepped off the planet Mars when he suggested that a parade was a waste of energy.

He had better things to do with his time than sit around discussing how to decorate the gym for the fall formal, or whether the yearbook that year would be red with black lettering or black with red lettering. Talk about a serious waste of time. Superficial City. Charlie hated that whole crowd.

But that didn't matter. After he finished giving the next car a jump-start, his shift would be over.

Freedom. No VW Bug, no Lilly Cameron. No problems. His older cousin Benny, who was a freshman at the technical college in town, would be taking over for the next shift. Charlie wasn't looking forward to seeing Benny, as much as he liked him, because Benny was going to ask him whether he'd found a date yet for their cousin Jack's wedding the next weekend. And Charlie was going to have to lie, again, and say he was "still evaluating his options." But the truth was, he didn't have a date, and he had no idea how he was going to get one.

But he absolutely had to. It was all part of a bet he had to win—unless he wanted to spend the first part of his summer vacation in Alaska with his strange aunt Margaret. Aunt Margaret was under the delusion that both Benny and Charlie, her "absolute favorite nephews," were dying to go on this trip to Alaska with her. When she'd offered to take one of them along, they'd both been too horrified to speak. Aunt Margaret had interpreted their silence as a sign that they were simply overwhelmed by the prospect of six nights and seven days on board a cruise ship, thousands of miles from home, with her.

Spending an afternoon—even a one-hour lunch— with Aunt Margaret was as painful as having a tooth drilled without any Novocain or nitrous oxide. There was no way Charlie could handle an entire week in captivity with Aunt Margaret. He knew she meant well, but as much as he wanted to see Alaska, he'd live without it if it meant playing checkers and shuffleboard on the deck of the ship.

Two weeks earlier, when they had made their bet, Charlie had assumed he'd win easily, and Benny would be the one on the Aloha Deck with their aunt. Charlie knew he was no Ethan Hawke, but he was certainly better-looking than his cousin. And Benny could be pretty obnoxious, too—his idea of a fun time would be having his date cheer him on at the go-cart track.

But now there was only a week left before Jack's wedding, and Charlie had yet to find a date. Of course, he hadn't exactly tried hard. But the two girls he'd asked the day before had turned him down, saying they already had plans. Maybe he'd waited too long, but *he* never made plans more than a week ahead. Why had everyone else?

Then a thought struck him like a bolt of lightning. Lilly Cameron needed her car fixed. He needed a date. They were both in desperate situations. Okay, maybe hers was more desperate, but his was still lousy. He could trade a quick car repair for a date to the wedding. They'd both be happy—or at least not miserable. It was worth a shot.

Of course, after the way he'd just left her there in the rain, he wasn't sure if she'd even listen to his proposal. He hoped she hadn't called another repair shop yet. He'd have to drive fast if he wanted to catch her. The person who was waiting for the jump-start would just have to find some jumper cables and do it himself. Charlie had a cruise to get out of!

"What do you think you're doing?"

Lilly wiped the sweat off her forehead with the sleeve of her blue sweatshirt. She'd been so busy trying to fix the bumper, she hadn't even heard the tow truck pull up beside her. She looked up and saw Charlie Roark standing there, staring down at her with an amused look on his face.

"Trying to fix this, since you won't help me," she said. "Not that you care."

"Move over, it'll never work that way." Charlie crouched down beside her, his work boots squishing in the mud.

As he grabbed the bumper his arm lightly brushed against Lilly's, and she felt an odd tingle inside. Charlie was in pretty good shape, in a wiry kind of way. *What's wrong with me?* she wondered. *Stop checking him out and start begging him to fix the car. Don't forget, Charlie Roark is a loser!* Then she noticed a small smear of grease on her sweatshirt from where Charlie's arm had touched her. Normally she would have been upset, but at that moment she didn't care if *all* her clothes were covered in grease. All she cared about was getting Sweetpea fixed.

Charlie pulled at the bumper a few times, but with no luck. "Maybe if we both pull at the same time, we'll get this sign loose," he said. "Okay with you?"

"Sure." Lilly wrapped her hands around the

signpost, which was still lodged firmly in the bumper, and Charlie got a grip on it as well.

Charlie braced his shoes against one of the front tires. "Ready? One, two, three—pull."

Lilly, pulling as hard as she could, felt a trickle of sweat—or was it rain?—roll down her neck and down the middle of her back. Charlie grunted as he dug his boots into the ground for one last pull and—

"Aargh!"

The sign came free, and Charlie toppled backward into the mud, his arms flailing, as if he were doing the backstroke in a pool.

Lilly collapsed onto the ground beside him. "We did it!" she said happily. "We might be covered in mud, but we did it."

"That sign was jammed in tight, all right. You really bashed into it, didn't you?" Charlie said.

"Yes, I really bashed into it. Are you happy?" Lilly was annoyed. But then she decided to change her tune. She needed Charlie's help, so she had to try to be nice. "So—you came back. Does that mean you're going to fix Sweetpea this weekend?" she asked hopefully.

"Sweetpea?" he asked.

"Yeah, that's what my dad calls the car. Pretty strange, huh?"

"I'll say."

"So what about it? Will you fix her?" Lilly asked again.

Charlie just shook his head and pulled his cap back over his head. He pointed to the still-bent bumper. "Not necessarily. Now that we've gotten it free from the stop sign, I can tow it. But we still have to check out the frame, realign the bumper—"

"Look, I know it's a lot of work, and I wouldn't ask unless I had to." Lilly bit her lip. "Isn't there *any* way you can bend the rules, just for me? Work overtime or something? I'm *really* in trouble here, Charlie. I mean, my father's going to go ballistic. My parents aren't going to trust me with anything ever again. I really messed up." Her voice was quivering, and she was afraid she was going to cry.

"Actually, I think I might be able to do it this weekend after all," Charlie said quickly.

"Really?" She knew she sounded desperate, but that was how she felt. Maybe Charlie did have a heart, after all.

"Well, that depends on you. After I drove away, I got this idea. It involves me helping you . . . and you helping me. A trade, actually," Charlie said.

Lilly picked one sneakered foot out of the mud—it made a loud slurping sound—and stepped closer to Charlie. "A trade? Not a car trade, I hope. Because that won't work for a second. My dad really knows this car. It's kind of sick, actually."

"No. Not a car trade." Charlie looked very nervous all of a sudden. He fiddled with a rope bracelet on his wrist. "I need something and you need something. So I thought . . . maybe we can help each other out. If you're willing."

"Of course I'm willing. I'll do anything. I mean,

look at me—I'm desperate. Please, Charlie, just tell me what it is," Lilly begged.

Charlie cleared his throat. "What I'm going to offer you isn't so terrible. I mean, I'm sure it's not the best thing that's ever come your way, but it could be fun."

"Charlie, spit it out already!" Lilly demanded. "What are you talking about?"

"Okay, here's the deal. I'll fix your car by to-morrow night if—"

"If I pay you triple double overtime?" Lilly interrupted.

"If you go on a date with me," Charlie said.

Lilly was too surprised to say anything at first, though she did hear herself utter a small noise that sounded like a laugh. Go on a date with Charlie Roark? Mr. I'm-too-environmentally-conscious-to-be-in-a-parade? The guy who'd just met her and already insulted her about ten times? "What are you talking about?" she exclaimed.

"A date. To a wedding next weekend. You know, you and me, going together."

"I know what a date is," Lilly snapped. "I didn't know you did, though."

"Hey, just because I don't go on tons of dates doesn't mean I'm—I'm . . . un-datable," Charlie said. "I'm very choosy, that's all. Anyway, it's just that this wedding . . . well, I made a bet with my cousin about bringing a date. If I don't show up with a girl, I'll lose."

"What's the bet for?" Lilly asked. She didn't like

the idea of being part of any bet. "And how is your cousin involved?"

"It's too complicated to go into right now," Charlie said. "And I have to get the tow truck back or my dad will be wondering what happened to me. But here's the deal. I fix the car, you come to the wedding—simple as that. So . . . what do you say?"

"I . . ." Lilly looked at the car, then at Charlie, then back at the car. Charlie wasn't exactly her idea of a great date—he was good-looking, in a strange kind of way, but he sure didn't hang around with anyone she knew. He seemed like a loner, and they had nothing in common. What would they possibly talk about for more than five minutes? But on the other hand, if she didn't go, and if her dad found out about the car . . . "Just one date?" she asked Charlie.

He nodded. "Next Saturday afternoon, three o'clock until about seven."

"Four *hours?*" Lilly blurted out.

"Spending time with me isn't exactly a death sentence, you know," Charlie said, sounding annoyed. "You might even have a good time."

"Oh, sure. It sounds like a blast," Lilly said sarcastically. "Hanging out at a wedding where I don't know anybody . . . I *wouldn't* know anybody, would I?" she asked worriedly.

"No, probably not," Charlie replied.

"Well, that helps, but—"

"Wait a second. Do you think you're too good to be seen with me?" Charlie asked.

"I—I'm not trying to be rude," Lilly stammered.

"Look, I don't have all day. What's your answer? Do you want to make the deal or not?" Charlie demanded, looking completely frustrated.

Lilly pictured her father's face when he saw the damage to Sweetpea. Then she imagined what he'd say about trust and communication and responsibility. "Yeah, I guess so. But you have to promise you'll have the car back by tomorrow night."

Charlie nodded. "And you have to promise you won't back out on me next Saturday." He held out his mud-spattered hand, and Lilly shook it, surprised by how strong a grasp he had. He started hitching Sweetpea to the tow truck, and Lilly watched him work. He seemed to be pretty good at what he was doing. She couldn't imagine having such a hard job—especially not while she was in school.

Charlie wiped his hands on his jeans and walked over to the driver's-side door. "Hey, do you want a ride home?"

"Yeah, whatever." Lilly shrugged.

"Don't get too excited about it. I'm only trying to do my job. But if you'd rather slog home through the mud, go ahead," Charlie said. "I wouldn't want to torture you by making you sit next to me." He opened the door and got into the truck.

"I'm going to have to sit next to you for four hours on Saturday," Lilly said. "I'd better get used to it."

Charlie started the truck. "You know, I'm already starting to regret that I made this deal with you."

"That makes two of us," Lilly said.

"Then you wouldn't want to spend any more

time with me than you absolutely have to, right?" Charlie called out over the top of the cab as Lilly began to walk around the truck to get in.

"That's for sure," Lilly said as Charlie revved the engine.

"In fact, I—"

"Then I'll just drop off the car tomorrow and spare you the pain. See you then!" Charlie slowly pulled the truck off the shoulder, turning left at the intersection.

"Wait! Wait up!" Lilly called. She started running after the truck, then stopped. There was no point.

For a minute she watched the banged-up front end of Sweetpea disappear backward down the road. Then she turned and started walking home in the opposite direction. That was when she remembered she'd left her jacket and her new sweater in the back seat of the car. All that for an outfit to wear, and now she didn't even have it.

But at the moment all she could think of was how grateful she was to Charlie. If he fixed Sweetpea as he'd promised, her father would never know what had happened. And if he didn't fix the car, she was never going to forgive him.

On the long, wet walk home, Lilly wondered why she'd never really noticed Charlie before or paid him any attention. It was true that he wasn't into the social scene, or at least not the same one she was into. But he was cute, even if he did act like a refugee from the sixties. There was something about Charlie that was different from the guys she normally hung out with. He hadn't once tried to impress her. She felt as though she could trust him to stick to their deal.

Even if he did act like a pompous jerk most of the time.

Chapter Four

"SO YOU WANT me to believe the girl who owns that VW over there just asked you out?" Charlie's cousin Benny shook his head. "No way. Not you."

"Maybe not to *you* . . ." Charlie smugly propped his feet on the desk in his uncle's office, stretching his arms over his head. His shift was finally over, and it was Benny's turn to drive the tow truck.

"And not to you, either," Benny said, frowning.

"What can I say? Some of us have it, and some of us don't," Charlie said.

"Yeah, and you *don't*," Benny said. He tapped a pencil with *Roark's Auto Body* printed on the side of it against the desk in the garage office. Benny's father owned the garage with Charlie's dad—they were brothers, and their sister was

Charlie and Benny's aunt Margaret. "So tell me what really happened."

"You don't need to know what really happened—it's personal. Just take note of the fact that I have a date for Jack's wedding. And as far as I can tell, you don't." Charlie smiled.

He was trying to sound confident, but the truth was, he was pretty nervous about his date with Lilly. He didn't really know anything about her—except that she was one of the most popular girls in school—and she didn't know anything about him. From the way things had gone that afternoon, he was afraid she might make him look like a total fool at the wedding.

"Look, Frisbee Man, I've known you long enough to know that dates don't just *happen* to you," Benny said. He took a sip of the coffee he'd just poured and made a face. "Ugh—I think this coffee's been on the burner since Thursday."

"Probably," Charlie said. "You could make a new pot, but then you'd have to get up off your butt."

"Actually, I'm waiting for someone to call for a tow so I can pick up some food," Benny said. "I'd kill for some onion rings from the drive-through right now."

Charlie shook his head. "You're such a dedicated employee. Well, I'd better get to work. Maybe you should spend your time finding someone to go out with next Saturday—unless you just want to concede right now."

"I'm not giving up, if that's what you're thinking,"

Benny said. "And I'll find a date. It's just that every girl I've asked happens to be busy next Saturday, that's all."

"Right," Charlie said. "Whatever you say."

"And when I do get a date, you can bet it'll be someone special," Benny said. "I'm not going to date just anybody—I'm looking for the perfect girl."

"Benny, I don't want to hear about your requirements for this nonexistent girl," Charlie said, getting up from his chair. "And if I were you, I'd start working pretty hard on finding a date, or else you're going to be seal-watching with Aunt Margaret faster than you can say Boredom Queen Cruise Line. Of course, that's not my problem, since I already have a date for next Saturday."

Benny just glowered at him. "Where are you going?"

"I told this girl—you know, the one I have a *date* with—that I'd fix her car this weekend," Charlie said. "She was so upset, I couldn't resist. In a little trouble with her dad—you know the routine."

"So how *did* you get a date so fast? Do you know her from school?" Benny asked, looking puzzled.

"Oh, yeah. We go way back." Charlie smiled. *Way back to half an hour ago, when we made this deal.* "We've known each other for a while, but the romance just kind of took off recently," he told Benny. *Right after she smashed into that stop sign, anyway.*

"Does she have a name?" Benny asked. "You haven't mentioned it yet, so I'm starting to wonder if she really exists."

"Lilly," Charlie said. "Lilly Cameron. You'll meet her next weekend." He grinned.

"It had to be luck," Benny replied, just as the phone rang. "There's no other explanation." He grabbed the phone. "Roark's Auto Body, how may I help you?"

Charlie opened the door of the office and went into the garage. One date with Lilly Cameron and he'd be off the hook for the cruise. He still couldn't believe he'd be going out with her. He couldn't even imagine what they'd talk about for more than two minutes, they had so little in common. He liked to hang out with his friends at Callaway Coffeehouse, and she spent her weekends at Sandy's, a burger-and-fries joint. He played Ultimate Frisbee, she was a cheerleader. They didn't have one single friend, thought, or interest in common.

But he didn't have to get along with her, he reminded himself as he began to work on the Bug. At least not longer than an afternoon. It wouldn't be that bad—especially when he had a week with Auntie M. to compare it to. Nothing Lilly said or did could be half as painful.

"You did not," Tracy said loudly to Lilly, trying to be heard above the noise of the party.

Lilly nodded. "I did."

"Are you serious?" Tracy looked more closely at Lilly, staring straight into her eyes.

"Stop it!" Lilly said, backing away. "Yes, I'm

31

serious. I know it's weird, but I had to do something!"

"Something, yeah. But that? I mean, why didn't you just call me?" Tracy asked. She stepped back to let someone pass by. The party was a blast. Nicole's house was filled with people, some munching on snacks, others dancing in the living room.

"You were busy looking after your brothers, remember? And you don't know how to fix cars. Charlie does," Lilly said with a shrug.

"Yeah, he knows how to fix cars and how to be a royal jerk," Tracy said. "Don't you remember how obnoxious he was at that council meeting last year? Like somebody died and made him president of the school. He didn't even run for student council and all of a sudden he wanted to decide what we did for the parade."

"I know. I remember that, okay? Listen, I didn't say I liked him. I didn't say I *wanted* to go out with him. And I sure didn't say I'd do it more than once, did I?" Lilly argued. "It's just a deal. It's called saving my butt. You know how my dad is about that car. I can't let him know what happened, that I drove Sweetpea without his permission—ever."

Tracy chewed on the lip of the empty plastic cup she was holding. "You're right about that. Your dad would go crazy if he found out you even sat in his car without him there. I mean, the dashboard's like a shrine as far as he's concerned. But I don't know . . . going out with Charlie Roark just seems a little drastic."

"No, wrecking my dad's car is drastic. This one-date deal is going to be a cinch compared to facing my dad." Lilly took a large tortilla chip from the bowl on the table and crunched into it. "How bad can it be? We'll be at the ceremony, then we'll eat at the reception, and then he'll bring me home." She gestured with the tortilla chip. "End of story."

"I guess so. But I'm glad it's not me. Hey, look who just walked in." Tracy gestured over Lilly's head.

Lilly turned around and faced the doorway. Bryan Bassani was taking off his jacket, hanging it on the coatrack by the door. He wore a rugby-striped sweater, jeans, and loafers. His black hair was slicked back, as usual. He turned toward Lilly and smiled for a second, revealing his perfectly white, straight teeth.

After her insane day, Lilly had almost forgotten Bryan would be at the party. She waved at him. Bryan waved back, then turned to talk to a group of guys near the doorway, friends of his she recognized from the soccer team.

"He is cute," Tracy said, "but he's also a snob."

"Not really. I mean, he just said hello to me and we barely even know each other," Lilly said. She wasn't sure how much she liked Bryan yet, but he did interest her more than the rest of the guys at school. There was something exciting about Bryan, something mysterious. Then again, she didn't exactly know anything about Charlie Roark, either—and she wasn't sure if she wanted to, even if he was kind of cute.

"Well, why don't you go talk to Bryan?" Tracy asked. "Why don't you admit you want to get to know him?"

Lilly shrugged. When Tracy rolled her eyes at her, Lilly laughed and added, "Okay, so maybe I've been talking about him a lot. It's not like I'm in love with him."

"Not yet, anyway." Tracy grinned. "Maybe after talking to him for a couple of minutes—"

"Tracy, I do not get infatuated that fast, unlike *some* people I know," Lilly interrupted. Tracy had been "falling in love" every other week for the past two years. "But don't worry—if I do fall in love with Bryan, you'll be the first to know." She smiled at Tracy and headed over to talk to a group of her friends from cheerleading.

Lilly wasn't like Tracy. She'd gone on dozens of dates and had yet to meet the right guy. Of course Lilly wanted to fall in love, but she wasn't going to force the issue. She knew it didn't happen that way. One day the right guy would walk into her life, and that would be that. And Bryan just might be the right guy. She'd simply have to wait and see.

"Hey, what's up?" she asked Kelly Costello. Kelly was a junior, too, and one of her best friends on the cheerleading squad.

"Hi, Lilly. We're just talking about the parade. Do you know when they'll reschedule it?" Kelly asked.

"I don't know, but thank God Nicole didn't cancel this party, too," Lilly said.

"No kidding," Kelly said. "I didn't get out of the house all day until this. How about you?"

Lilly smiled, her mouth half-crinkling into a smile. "No, I didn't go anywhere. Not really."

"Weren't you bored to death?" Kelly groaned. "I've never gotten all my homework done on a Saturday before. Ever. What did you do?"

"Nothing much," Lilly said. *Just smashed into a stop sign and practically ruined my life.* She thought about Charlie for a second, spending the night fixing Sweetpea instead of hanging around at a great party like this one. She realized he'd sacrificed his entire Saturday night for a date. Talk about desperate! She'd have to find out more about that bet. She didn't want to get involved in anything slimy.

But whatever the bet, she was glad for it—otherwise she'd be home, figuring out ways to tell her father about his precious car. And about how she'd broken his first rule of parenting: responsibility. And the second one: trust. And the third, and the fourth . . .

Lilly snapped out of her thoughts and caught the end of a conversation taking place behind her. It seemed as if a few girls she didn't know very well were talking about some guy.

"I don't know. I think Charlie's so cute, but he never comes to any parties. How am I supposed to talk to him if he's never around?"

Charlie? Lilly thought. *Are they talking about Charlie Roark?*

"He hangs out at that coffeehouse on Main Street

a lot," the other girl said. "You could start going there, I guess. I wonder why he's such a loner."

Because he works all the time, Lilly was tempted to turn around and say. What was this, Charlie Roark Day? She'd never even noticed him before, and suddenly he was everywhere. Girls actually had crushes on him. "Hard to believe," she muttered to herself.

"What did you say?" Kelly asked her.

"Oh, uh, nothing," Lilly told her.

Kelly gave her a contemplative look. "You're not yourself tonight—you're so quiet. Is everything okay?"

"Oh, sure. Everything's great." Lilly smiled weakly. As soon as Charlie got Sweetpea back in excellent shape, everything would be great. As soon as her parents got home, noticed nothing, and she could get back to her normal life, she would live happily ever after.

And if Charlie Roark didn't keep his end of the bargain, she was going to make his life completely miserable.

The same way her dad would make hers.

Chapter Five

B Y FIVE O'CLOCK Sunday afternoon Lilly was pacing the kitchen floor, praying Charlie would bring Sweetpea home before her parents arrived. Suddenly the doorbell rang. "Finally!" she said as she ran to answer the door.

Charlie stood on the front step. "Uh, hey, how's it going?" he asked, sounding a little nervous.

Without saying a word, Lilly pushed him aside and stepped onto the front walkway, trying to get a look at the car.

"Well, excuse *me*," Charlie said, practically falling as he took a step backward into the yard.

"Sorry," Lilly said, "but I'm kind of nervous, if that's okay with you." She walked over to the car parked in the driveway and crouched down in front, studying it from every angle. She felt like one of those golfers she'd watched during her boring

37

TV marathon the day before, setting up a long putt on the eighteenth green.

"Well?" Charlie had followed her every step, and now he leaned against the driver's-side door. "Is it okay?"

"Is it okay? It's incredible!" Lilly exclaimed, giving Charlie a quick hug. It felt surprisingly good. "I can't tell anything ever happened." *What's gotten into me?* she wondered. *Did I really just hug Charlie Roark—and like it?*

"You don't have to sound so surprised," Charlie said. "I told you I'd fix it."

"I know you *told* me that, but I wasn't sure you could actually do it," Lilly admitted.

"Yeah, that's right. My dad hires only really incompetent people to work for him," Charlie said. "He's trying to run his business into the ground."

"Come on, I didn't mean it like that," Lilly said.

"Yes, you did," Charlie said. "On top of my fine auto-repair skills, I'm pretty good at sensing distrust in people's voices."

"Look, all I meant was, I thought it might be trashed for good. Do you think I know anything about fixing cars?"

"Well, I know you don't know how to drive one," Charlie said with a smirk.

Lilly folded her arms across her chest and sighed loudly. "I think we covered my driving record yesterday."

"Right," Charlie said. "Sorry."

Lilly stared at his wildly colored tie-dyed T-shirt, overalls, and lowtop Converse sneakers. Purple Converse sneakers. This guy had no fashion sense whatsoever. "So . . . thanks for doing such a good job. I guess I'll see you at school."

"Yeah, definitely," Charlie said. "And next Saturday. Don't forget."

"Oh, I haven't forgotten." Lilly looked at Charlie's ponytail and the five or six rope bracelets around his wrist as he bent down to tie one of his shoelaces. "Are you sure you wouldn't rather just have cash?" she asked. "I mean, not that I could pay you a lot, but we could set up a payment plan—"

"No, absolutely not," Charlie said, standing up. "Just the one date is perfect. You'll really be helping me out."

Lilly shrugged. "Okay, whatever." Even if she'd never go out with Charlie in the normal scheme of things, how bad could one afternoon be?

"I'll be out of here in a second. My cousin Benny should be here any minute now to pick me up. I can just wait out here," Charlie said.

"That's stupid. Why don't you come inside? My parents won't be home for another couple of hours," Lilly said.

Charlie's eyebrows shot up, and they exchanged awkward glances. Then he followed her into the house and she got two glasses out of the cupboard. She was about to pour diet cola into each when Charlie said, "Just water for me, please."

"You sure you don't want something else?" Lilly

asked. "We have other things. Juice, root beer, Fruity Fun Drink—"

"Fruity Fun Drink? I didn't know anyone still drank that stuff," Charlie said. "Isn't it toxic?"

"Well, my dad's been drinking it since, like, 1968, so I don't think so." Lilly frowned at him.

"Water would be great, thanks," Charlie said awkwardly.

Lilly stepped toward him and handed him the empty glass. If this was any indication of how their date was going to go, it would be one long afternoon. "There's the sink if you want some water." She pointed at the faucet. "Help yourself."

Suddenly the sound of a loud, blaring horn came from the front of the house. Lilly nearly jumped, it was so loud.

"That must be Benny," Charlie said.

Lilly nodded. *Of course. Rudeness obviously runs in the family,* she thought. She walked over to the front door and opened it. "Thanks for bringing the car over."

Charlie handed her the empty glass. "Sure. And thanks for agreeing to next weekend."

"Hey, that's what I wanted to ask you about. What exactly are the—"

"Hi there!" An older-looking boy with a blond buzz cut leaned out the window of a beat-up red car and waved at Lilly. "So you're the girl who's dating Charlie, huh?"

"Dating Charlie?" Lilly asked.

Charlie cleared his throat. "Well, uh, take care."

He squeezed Lilly's arm and then jogged over toward Benny's car.

"Yeah," Benny said. "He's told me all about you. Hey, I'll see you next weekend, right?"

"Right," Lilly said slowly. "Next weekend."

As Benny backed the car out of the driveway, Charlie waved to Lilly. She waved back as they drove off down the street, wondering what he'd meant. *The girl who's dating Charlie?* One date didn't quite count as "dating," especially when they hadn't even had it yet. Then she wondered what it would be like to date Charlie. He certainly was cute. He was just terribly obnoxious, too.

One date, she reminded herself as she settled Sweetpea back in the garage, where it should have stayed all weekend. She rubbed the front bumper in the middle, and it was as smooth as could be. No one would ever know it had once been terribly crumpled.

She didn't know what Charlie would be like on their date, but he certainly was good at fixing cars. She was actually a little surprised by how professional the job looked. Charlie had kept his end of the bargain—now she had to keep hers.

"She's cute. Way cuter than I expected," Benny said. "I had no idea you were bringing such a babe to the wedding."

"Neither did I," Charlie muttered under his breath.

"So, is this your first date with her? I mean,

why haven't you said anything about her before?" Benny asked.

Charlie shrugged and rolled down the window. "I just got to know her well recently." And the way she'd just treated him, he wasn't sure he wanted to know her any better! If she weren't so pretty, he might have told her to forget all about their deal. He'd always noticed Lilly at school—who didn't? She was popular and had lots of boyfriends. Charlie had never thought he'd have a real conversation with her, let alone go on a date with her.

"So why didn't you let me talk to her?" Benny slowed for a red light.

"Oh, uh . . . she's a little shy." Charlie pushed some cassettes and soda cans on the floor of the car out of the way of his feet. With all the junk, there was hardly any room left for him to get comfortable. "You know, this car is a total mess. I can't believe you keep it like this."

Benny turned left onto Charlie's street. "She didn't seem shy when she was waving. You know, she looked kind of familiar when she did that. Is she—"

"Yeah, she's a cheerleader," Charlie said. "They do that waving thing a lot."

"Charlie Roark dating a cheerleader." Benny shook his head. "Now I've seen everything."

"Well, we're not *dating* dating," Charlie said, then remembered the bet: in order to win, Charlie's date with Lilly had to seem real.

"Really? I thought—"

"What I mean is, we're really looking forward to

our *first* date, at the wedding." Benny stopped the car in front of Charlie's house, and Charlie opened the door. "Thanks a lot for the ride, Benji."

"Don't call me that," Benny said. "And take your hippie tapes with you." He tossed a few cassettes at Charlie, who caught one and dropped two. "Nice catch."

"See you around," Charlie said. "Benji."

"So how was your trip?" Lilly took a small duffel bag from her mother's hands and carried it into the living room.

"We had a wonderful time," her mother said. "But that drive is exhausting." She sank into the overstuffed floral chair by the fireplace. Mrs. Cameron had shoulder-length hair, dark brown like Lilly's. She was wearing a gray sweater and black jeans. "Next time we're going to fly."

"Next time it's their turn to come here," Lilly's father said. He set down their suitcase by the stairs and took a seat on the couch beside Lilly. Her father was forty-six and trying hard not to age—even though his hair was a bit thin, he still dressed in Levi's jeans and flannel shirts, like half the guys Lilly knew at school. "So what did you do all weekend?" he asked Lilly.

Lilly moved over on the couch. "Oh, not much." She tried to keep her nervousness from showing in her hands as she reached for a handful of nuts from the bowl on the table and put one in her mouth.

"Lilly, your hands are shaking," Mrs. Cameron said.

"Really? I'm just . . . tired." Lilly smiled. She felt as if she was about to blow the whole thing. She'd never kept things from her parents before— nothing major like this, anyway. It was making her incredibly uncomfortable.

"Too bad that parade was canceled," her father said. "What did you do all day? I heard the weather was pretty bad up here."

"Oh, yeah," Lilly said anxiously. "It was incredibly bad weather. In fact, it rained all day. I went for a walk and got totally soaked." *My jacket!* Lilly suddenly remembered she'd left it and her new sweater in Sweetpea's back seat before Charlie towed the car away. "I bet you guys are thirsty. Want something to drink? I'll get it." She hopped up from the couch. "Orange juice okay?"

"That sounds wonderful," her mother said, stretching her legs out in front of her.

Lilly went into the kitchen and took out some glasses. She listened briefly to her parents talking in the living room before she quickly opened the door to the garage, slipped out, quietly opened Sweetpea's door, and grabbed her jacket and the bag from the department store. Then she crouched down in front of the car and ran her hand over the bumper one last time. No marks other than the normal wear and tear of nearly thirty years—no dents, nothing. She breathed a sigh of relief.

She crept back into the kitchen, poured the orange juice, and went back into the living room. "Here you go." She handed each of her parents a glass.

"What service." Her father smiled. "It's good to be home."

"Did I hear you go into the garage for something?" Mrs. Cameron asked.

Lilly nearly choked on the juice in her mouth. She cleared her throat before answering, "Yeah, I . . . left my jacket out there to dry yesterday and I forgot to bring it in. You know, my short tan jacket that's supposed to be good in bad weather, only it doesn't really do anything. When we were talking about the weather, I remembered I'd been wearing it when I went for that walk. It's not even dry yet, that's how wet I got. I think I need a new spring jacket, something more like a raincoat. Maybe they're on sale now. What do you think?"

"Oh. Maybe." Mrs. Cameron shrugged. "I was just afraid we'd left the lights on."

"Oh," Lilly said. *And there I was, babbling like an idiot about my jacket.* She was going to have to be careful that she didn't give herself away by acting so nervous.

There's nothing to worry about, she told herself. Her father had parked their Toyota next to Sweetpea, he'd walked past it, even looked right at it, and he hadn't noticed anything. There wasn't anything *to* notice, she reminded herself. And once she got through her date with Charlie Roark, the whole thing was going to be a distant memory. No one would ever have to know what had happened.

Especially not her parents.

45

Chapter Six

"MY PARENTS DIDN'T suspect a thing," Lilly confidently told Tracy the next morning as they stood on the front steps of the school building. "My dad even drove me to school this morning in Sweetpea."

"And he didn't notice anything?" Tracy asked, shifting her backpack to her other shoulder.

"No. I told you, Charlie did a really good job," Lilly said. "I even watched my dad run a cloth over the hood, like he does every Monday—part of his weird love-of-car ritual. Then he didn't notice anything the entire drive here. And he knows that car better than he knows my mother."

"Well, at least Charlie Roark's good for something besides just hanging around." Tracy shook her head and pointed to a group of guys standing over by the statue of the school's first principal, Harry F. Loftus.

Everyone joked about the statue being ridiculous—it was nicknamed The Harry—since the school had only been built in 1979. It wasn't anything truly historical yet but, Lilly guessed, eventually it would be. Maybe in 2079, if it was still around.

"What is he *doing?*" Lilly asked as she watched Charlie leap up onto the side of the statue and bounce something off his knee onto the figure of Harry F. Loftus, then off his thigh and back over toward the group.

"They're playing Hacky-sack," Tracy said as they walked around to a spot beside the front steps where all the popular kids—namely, everyone Lilly knew—hung out before the first bell for homeroom.

"It seems like a pretty stupid game to me," Lilly said. "What do you do, just bounce that thing around on your feet?"

"I'm not sure, exactly," Tracy admitted.

"Hey, do me a favor," Lilly said, changing the subject. "Don't tell anyone about what happened with the car or about the date I have with Charlie for Saturday, okay?"

"Sure. Why don't you want anyone to know?"

"For one thing, the more people who know, the bigger the chance it'll eventually get back to my parents. Someone could slip and say something. And for another . . ."

"If someone found out you were dating Charlie, they might not ask you out? Someone standing right over there?" Tracy said, pointing toward Bryan Bassani.

Lilly nodded. "Exactly." She'd had a good time talking with Bryan at Nicole's party, and she didn't want her arranged date with Charlie to get in the way of any developing romance between herself and Bryan.

"Your secrets are safe with me," Tracy said, just as they joined their group of friends.

A few minutes later Lilly was casually talking to Kelly and her boyfriend, Jake, when something soft hit her on the back. She turned and saw a small, square beanbag lying on the ground.

"Could you help us out here?" one of the boys in Charlie's group called over to her.

She looked down at the Hacky-sack, and then over at the group of guys. What did they expect her to do, get into the game and bounce it off her foot? She turned back around and continued talking to Jake about the upcoming spring formal, which the student council was still trying to organize. Jake was the student council treasurer, in addition to being co-captain of the baseball team.

"Well, we have enough money to rent a large space, but I think we should just have it here," Jake said. "That way we can use the extra money to hire a great band."

"We should have an all-school vote on it," Lilly said, "and find out if people would rather have a new location or a cool band."

Lilly heard something rustle and sensed someone behind her. She turned around. Charlie was picking up the Hacky-sack.

"Thanks for your help." He smiled at her as he straightened up. "We really appreciated it."

Lilly smiled back evenly. "Sure. Anytime. Oh, and I forgot to tell you yesterday—thanks for giving me a ride home the other day. You know, when I was stranded in the pouring rain."

"No problem," Charlie said. "Just glad I could help." He brushed off his hands on his jeans and ran back over to his friends.

Lilly turned back to Jake, but he was busy talking to Kelly.

"What was that all about?" Tracy asked. "I thought you guys were friends now."

"No, we're definitely not *friends*," Lilly said. "Why should we be?"

"Your date's certainly going to be a blast," Tracy said, rolling her eyes.

"Tell me about it." Lilly shook her head as the bell rang. Halfway up the steps, there was the usual traffic jam of everyone trying to get through the doors at once. Lilly paused for a second, and realized Charlie and his friends were behind her.

"So what do you say, man—you playing with us this Saturday?"

"I can't do anything this Saturday," Charlie's voice replied.

"Are you working again?"

"No, nothing that good. I have to go to my cousin's wedding." He groaned.

"A wedding? Are you serious?"

"Yeah. And it gets worse. . . . I have to bring a

49

date," Charlie said. "Kind of a blind date, actually."

"Good luck, man. Wouldn't want to be you," his friend replied.

"I know. It's going to be a total drag," Charlie said. "But you gotta do what you gotta do, right?"

Lilly felt like turning around and stuffing that silly little beanbag down Charlie's throat. *A total drag?* For one thing, no one but her father even used terms like that anymore. And as far as she was concerned, no one was allowed to unless they'd grown up in the sixties. And for another, it had been Charlie's idea to bring her on this date, not hers. He didn't have to make it sound like it would be so horrible.

Sure, it *would* be terrible—for her! Having to hang out with a guy who thought it was cool to jump around with a beanbag on his knee in front of school, a guy who wore tie-dyed T-shirts and purple sneakers, a guy who never went to parties and didn't know any popular people.

Remember Sweetpea, Lilly told herself. *You did this all for Sweetpea.*

A total drag, Lilly wrote in her notebook during English class. *Definition: having a date with someone who thinks he's superior and acts like a jerk.*

She gave Charlie a sideways glance and noticed how cute he was when he wasn't insulting her. She'd never paid any attention to him in class, and now she was painfully aware of the fact that he sat only three rows over from her—way too close for comfort.

Definition, she wrote. *Wrecking your dad's car and having to pay with your life.*

Okay, maybe it wasn't her life. But close enough.

Mrs. Vaughn was talking about how to write the perfect essay, and how nobody had even come close on their last papers. "All year I've been telling you the same thing—organize your thoughts. I've photocopied a paper that does a very good job of incorporating a lot of information into a tight, well-organized essay. I'd like you all to read it as an example of what you should be doing." Mrs. Vaughn handed the papers to the first person in each row.

Lilly was glancing at the essay when she heard Mrs. Vaughn say, "Nice job." She turned to see whom Mrs. Vaughn was complimenting and was shocked to find her standing beside Charlie's desk.

I shouldn't be that surprised, she thought. *He's the one who bragged to me about all his honors classes.* She was impressed, though. Charlie obviously put in a lot of hours at his father's garage, and he still found the time to do well in school.

That's because he doesn't have a life! Charlie never does anything remotely fun, she thought, still looking over at him. Unless, of course, you counted hanging around with a bunch of losers and playing stupid games as doing something.

Charlie suddenly turned his head and caught

Lilly staring at him. He smiled briefly at her and shrugged, as if to say, "I can't help it if I'm a genius."

He thinks he's so great! Lilly turned her attention back to his paper, determined to find something wrong with it. Anything. She skimmed for typos Mrs. Vaughn might have missed. Nothing. She read it through—it was all about new alternative energy sources, of course—and found that it flowed just as naturally as Mrs. Vaughn said it did. He presented quite a convincing argument.

She stared at the *A* written at the top. Then Mrs. Vaughn placed her paper in front of her. *B— needs further development. A bit sketchy at times. You need to spend more time developing your argument.*

I don't have more time! Lilly frowned. *Some of us have a social life.*

When she looked up from reading over her essay, Lilly noticed Charlie watching her, a conceited look on his face. It was one thing to be a good student, but totally gross to brag about it. He was probably feeling extra smug that week, if that was possible, since he'd railroaded her into that date. Sure, he'd told his friends it would be a total drag, but Lilly knew that he was thrilled to get a date with her—or he should be, anyway. Charlie's friends would have to be impressed when he told them he was dating her. He knew it and she knew it.

Lilly suddenly realized she didn't know what

Charlie expected of her on this date—he'd never explained the specifics of the bet. It was time to make a few things clear.

"Psst."

Charlie looked over to his right. Hilary Jones was holding out a folded piece of paper to him. When Mrs. Vaughn turned to write something on the board, he quickly grabbed the note.

DATE RULES! was written in capital letters at the top of the sheet. *Number one: You will not tell anyone that I am going to this wedding with you. Number two: You will bring me home at seven o'clock sharp. I have plans afterward. Important plans. Number three: This is not your typical date. There will be no hand holding, no hugging, and absolutely NO KISSING!*

Charlie tried not to laugh out loud. Since when did he plan on *any* of the above? One: He wasn't about to tell his friends he was going out with Lilly Cameron. He'd never hear the end of the jokes if he did. Two: He didn't want to hang out with her any longer than he had to—he'd have her home by six, if they could skip out early. And three: He had absolutely no desire to get romantic with her. *Talk about your major-sized ego!*

Not everyone wanted to date Lilly Cameron, and it was about time she realized that. *She thinks she's so great.* Okay, so she was pretty—very pretty, in fact. She was a popular cheerleader and junior-class vice president of the student council. But Lilly needed to realize she wasn't everyone's idea of the perfect date! He would have made the same deal with any girl who was stranded on the side of the road. He was that desperate. With her ego, Lilly probably thought he'd just been cruising around in the tow truck looking for her so he could ask her out!

He took the cap off his pen, circled *NO KISS-ING,* and wrote, *Don't worry. And the same goes for you*—please *don't kiss me!*

He handed the note back to Hilary, who then passed it to Lilly. He watched her unfold the sheet of paper.

Lilly's face turned bright red as she crumpled the piece of paper into a ball and stuffed it into her book bag on the floor.

Serves her right if she's embarrassed, he thought, slouching back in his chair. She had some nerve, making a rule against kissing her. As if he'd been waiting his whole life for this one date with her. *I should have sent back my own rules,* Charlie thought. *Rule number one: Stop acting like such a princess!*

Chapter Seven

WHAT AM I *doing?* Lilly wondered. *I should be at the baseball game with everyone else.* She'd been standing outside her house, wearing a long blue and pink floral-print dress and high-heeled pumps, her hair brushed to perfection, her makeup nicely done, as usual, for the past fifteen minutes.

All dressed up and nowhere to go.

I wish.

Charlie was late, and with each minute that passed, Lilly fought the urge to run back into the house and hide in the closet before he actually showed up.

Lilly didn't feel up to acting nice and friendly—especially to Charlie. He could be such a jerk sometimes. She'd much rather spend the day with her friends, the people she really liked. The baseball team had a special doubleheader to make up for some rained-out games, and as co-captain of the pep squad, she really ought to be there, helping with the bake sale. It didn't make any sense.

She hadn't talked to Charlie all week, not since Monday, when they'd exchanged that note. That dumb note. Why had she written it in the first place? And why did he have to respond in such an obnoxious way?

Of course, they'd seen each other around at school, but they hadn't acknowledged each other. It was better that way, she decided. They'd probably have ended up arguing anyway.

So how were they going to get through an entire afternoon together? she wondered, pushing back a strand of hair that had blown into her face in the brisk April breeze. *Maybe his cousin and his fiancée eloped,* she thought. *It could happen.* But not with the way her luck had been going lately.

She heard an engine rev before she noticed a large truck tearing around the corner and down her street. *Oh, no,* she thought.

A beat-up red tow truck with *Roark's Auto Body* in flaky white script on the side pulled up right in front of her, and the passenger door swung open. "You ready?"

Charlie looked good in his black-and-white sports jacket, a white shirt, black pants, a colorful tie, and, of course, his usual Converse sneakers—only that day they were black instead of purple. She wondered if they were his formal sneakers, for special occasions. He looked handsome all dressed up. His dirty-blond hair wasn't in a ponytail for once, and it looked really nice brushed out over the lapel of his suit jacket. He looked like a guy she'd seen in a magazine ad for a hip men's clothing store.

As she stepped into the truck Lilly's dress got caught underneath her and almost snagged on the rough seat cover. "Hey, nice car," she said sarcastically, closing the door. She brushed a large crumb off the seat.

"I'm on call today. That's the problem with having a family business. When you have family events, someone always suffers. Today's not my lucky day," Charlie said, checking the side-view mirror.

"Mm," Lilly muttered, knowing exactly how he felt. It was definitely not her lucky day, either. "On call—is that like a doctor?"

Charlie drove away from the curb, flooring the accelerator, and suddenly jerked the truck around in a U-turn. A bottle of veggie juice on the dashboard in front of Charlie skidded over and flew into Lilly's lap. She grabbed it just as it flipped over, spilling several drops onto her dress.

"Nice move," she said, shooting Charlie a dirty look. "I just got tomato juice all over me."

"Sorry." Charlie didn't sound very sorry. "I think there's a rag behind the seat."

Lilly rummaged behind her and pulled out a large white rag—covered in oil and grease. "Oh, this is really going to help."

"Sorry." Charlie just kept driving.

Is that all he's going to say all afternoon? Lilly had always thought of him as the type to go on and on. He'd never been at a loss for words before—it was practically the only thing they had in common. Actually, it *was* the only thing they had in common.

Lilly found a small packet of tissues in her purse and dabbed at the spots of juice on her dress. She was thankful they hadn't fully soaked into the fabric yet. True, she wasn't going to know anyone at the wedding, but she didn't want everyone to think she was a slob.

Charlie whipped around the next corner just as quickly as he'd pulled the U-turn, then drove down the street twice as fast as Lilly would have. When they came to a stoplight, he waited until the last minute to apply the brakes. Then he floored the accelerator when the light turned green. *Talk about a bad driver,* Lilly thought with a grimace. She held the juice bottle out in front of her, the little juice that was left inside sloshing around in the bottom. "Do you have to drive so fast? Doesn't that waste energy?"

"I don't think you're the one who should be giving advice about driving," Charlie replied coolly. "Anyway, I'm only doing this because we're going to be late."

"Well, that's hardly my fault," Lilly said. "I was ready and waiting for you fifteen minutes ago."

"Something came up at home, okay?" Charlie suddenly sounded upset, so Lilly decided to back off. He was obviously in as rotten a mood as she was. Maybe even worse. But at least he wasn't saying it was her fault.

He leaned forward and turned up the radio. It was hard to hear over the loud engine, but Lilly knew that whatever song it was, she didn't like it. She slouched down and stared out the window. So far things were going just as she'd imagined—and they couldn't get much worse.

About fifteen minutes later they pulled up in front of the church. Charlie was halfway up the steps before he realized he'd forgotten about Lilly. He finally turned around and waited for her.

This date is going from bad to worse, she thought as they entered the church.

"Bride or groom?" a handsome usher asked them.

Charlie just stared at him. "Neither!"

"No, he means, which side do we want to sit on," Lilly said. "Groom, right?"

Charlie shrugged. "I guess."

The usher took her arm and they headed down the aisle. Lilly smiled at the usher as he stopped. "This okay?" he asked.

She nodded. "Thanks." She sat down next to Charlie, and turned to watch the usher go back up the aisle to greet other guests. *Come back!* she felt like yelling. *I'd rather be here with you!*

"What's taking them so long?" Charlie asked.

"They're probably getting their pictures taken," Lilly said, as if it were the most obvious thing in the world.

"What about us? I'm starving," Charlie said. He stared at the empty buffet table.

The reception was being held in his aunt Margaret's backyard, under a large yellow and white striped tent awning. There was a wood floor for dancing, a disc jockey and a table for his equipment, and lots of tables for people to sit at. The ceremony had ended a while before and all the guests had arrived from the church. But Jack and Lorraine—the bride and groom—and the rest of the wedding party were nowhere to be seen.

Charlie's stomach growled. He hadn't had time to eat lunch, and it was five o'clock already. "Aren't you hungry?" he asked Lilly.

"Kind of," she said. "You'd think they'd at least put out some appetizers."

"You'd think so, but Aunt Margaret doesn't do anything the way other people do," Charlie said. "She's kind of . . . odd, in a nice way. But definitely odd."

Speaking of his aunt Margaret, Charlie looked around for Benny. At the church, Charlie hadn't been able to tell if Benny was with a girl or not. *There's no way,* he thought, scanning the yard. As of Friday night, the last time he'd spoken to Benny, his cousin still hadn't found a date. And Charlie couldn't wait to see Benny so he could rub it in. Benny was going to be spending a torturous week in Alaska.

Lilly sighed and looked at her watch for the fiftieth time that afternoon. Charlie knew she was bored. He couldn't believe how great Lilly looked.

She'd gotten dressed so nicely for an arranged date with someone she didn't even like. She really looked fantastic. Maybe a little on the conservative side, but she couldn't help that. She was definitely one of the prettiest girls he'd ever known, much less dated. *Who are you kidding?* he asked himself. *This is practically your first date ever.*

A few minutes later, Jack and Lorraine arrived. Everyone stood and applauded when the disc jockey announced them, and then they danced their first dance as husband and wife. Charlie found the whole thing a little on the sappy side. He couldn't believe that his older cousin Jack, the guy who'd showed him how to skateboard and rock-climb, was the same person who was now wearing a tuxedo and dancing to an old Frank Sinatra tune. Something was very wrong with this picture.

Lilly turned to Charlie and sighed. "Weddings are so romantic, even when you don't know the people getting married," she said.

"I don't know," Charlie said, sitting down next to her. "Sometimes it seems like a big, elaborate pageant. Everyone's all dressed up in these costumes—the bridesmaids, the ushers, and especially the bride and groom."

Lilly seemed to be thinking it over. After a minute she replied, "I never looked at it that way before. But I still think they're fun. I guess I don't mind all that pageantry. Maybe it's just not your style. You know, you can make your wedding however you want it to be. There aren't any rules."

Charlie couldn't resist smiling at the mention of the word *rules*. It brought his thoughts back to their English class on Monday, and he remembered how red her face had turned when she read his note. "Do you think they let you get married in shorts?" he asked, putting his hand on the back of her chair.

"Only if you have matching sneakers," Lilly said, smiling. "Purple, right?"

"Definitely. What other color is there?" Charlie looked at her and smiled back. At least she had a good sense of humor. He had to give her that.

"Well, the formal black, of course." She pointed to his sneakers. "I can see you getting married on top of some mountain, after you make everyone hike up there. Or on a boat out in the middle of the ocean. Something weird," Lilly said.

"Those sound like cool ideas, actually, but I don't think I'll ever get married," Charlie said, shaking his head.

He was expecting Lilly to make some comment about how he'd hardly have a chance to get married if he had to barter his way into getting one lousy date, but she didn't. Instead, she just asked, "Really? Why not?"

"I don't know. It's just hard to imagine," Charlie said.

Lilly sighed. "Yeah, I know what you mean. I look at my parents, and I think they're so much older than me. Which they are, but, I mean, in so many ways. I can't imagine being all settled down the way they are—for the rest of their lives. But they're happy." Lilly shrugged. "Who knows? Maybe in ten years I'll want to settle down, too."

"Yeah, maybe. Kind of hard to picture getting married, going to work . . ."

"Owning a car," Lilly added.

Charlie laughed. "Yeah. For some of us that's *really* hard to picture."

"Hey, you don't have to keep bringing that up," Lilly said.

"Sorry. Couldn't resist. And I'm sorry I was so rude when I came to pick you up. Something really did come up at home." Charlie didn't want to go into any details with Lilly. He didn't feel he knew her well enough to tell her about his personal problems.

"That's okay. I've already forgotten about it," Lilly said, smiling.

She looked so beautiful, Charlie wanted to lean over and kiss her, rules or no rules. He ought to, he thought—just to serve her right for making it a rule *not* to. He couldn't believe he was actually having a hard time resisting the urge to kiss her.

"Hey, Lilly," he said. "Remember that sheet of—"

"Charlie! My man," a loud male voice interrupted.

Charlie turned around to find Benny walking toward him, a huge smile on his face. He was wearing a navy-blue pin-striped suit, and he looked like he'd gotten a new buzz cut just for the occasion. His blond hair was shining in the late afternoon sun. And he looked one hundred percent *alone*.

"Benj—Benny, what's up?" Charlie stood up

just in time for Benny to clap him on the back. An ex-wrestler and football tackle, Benny was still very strong. Charlie grinned. "Where have you been hiding yourself?" *As if I don't know he's been hiding from me because he doesn't have a date.*

"Oh, just had to make a few stops on the way over here," Benny said. "Hi." He held out his hand to Lilly. "We didn't get the chance to meet properly the other day."

Charlie just stared at him. Since when was his cousin this polite?

"Hi. I'm Lilly."

"So I've heard. Are you having a good time?" Benny asked. "Is there anything I can get you?"

I hope he doesn't think that if he steals my date, she counts as his date, too, Charlie thought. "Yeah, you can bring both of us some food, now that they're finally starting to bring it out," Charlie said.

"I asked Lilly, not you," Benny said. "And balancing three plates is going to be hard enough."

"So don't eat so much," Charlie said. "Have one plate like the rest of us."

"Only one plate's for me. The other's for Sheila. Here she is now." He waved at a girl who was walking out of the house and onto the deck. She waved back and headed toward the three of them.

"Sheila? Who's Sheila?" Charlie demanded.

"My date, of course." Benny turned to Charlie, rubbed his hands together, and grinned. "So. I guess that makes us even?"

"Even?" Lilly asked. "What are you talking about?"

"Look, there's my dad," Charlie said, standing up and grabbing Lilly's hand just as Sheila approached the group. "Tell Sheila we'll meet her later." If Benny found out that Lilly knew anything about the bet and had agreed to come with him only because she had no choice, Charlie would probably lose. "Come on, I want to introduce you to him."

"Well, okay. Sure," Lilly said, glancing down at his hand clasped around hers.

What am I doing? he wondered. Self-conscious, he let her hand go, and the two of them made their way across the lawn.

Lilly walked beside Charlie, scanning the guests' tables to see if she could find Charlie's father before she was introduced. *This is kind of fun,* she thought, *meeting Charlie's family, even if I don't plan on ever seeing him again.*

A woman stepped right in front of them, and almost bumped right into Lilly. "Charlie!" She planted a huge kiss on his cheek.

"Aunt Margaret." Charlie leaned backward as his aunt wrapped her arms around his waist. She was wearing a shiny bright-purple dress, and she had a multicolored scarf around her neck. Lilly thought she must be about fifty. Her hair was dyed an unnatural orange-red.

"And who's your lovely guest?" The woman beamed at Lilly.

"This is Lilly Cameron," Charlie said. "Lilly,

this is my aunt Margaret—Jack's mother."

"It's very nice to meet you," Lilly said.

"Oh, the pleasure is all mine." Aunt Margaret kept beaming at Lilly. "What a lovely, lovely dress."

"Thank you," Lilly said.

"I had no idea Charlie had someone so special in his life."

He doesn't! At least not after seven o'clock this evening, Lilly thought, but she forced herself to smile politely.

"Charlie, you've been holding out on me," Aunt Margaret said, wagging her finger at him as if she were scolding him. "Dating somebody without telling me is a no-no."

"Well . . . I . . ." Charlie's face turned red.

"I'm sure he meant to tell you about us," Lilly said. "It's just kind of sudden, that's all." She heard Charlie sigh with relief.

"Isn't that just like love?" Aunt Margaret shook her head. "One day you're going about your life, and the next, well, it hits you like a freight train."

Like a stop sign, you mean, Lilly thought, trying not to laugh.

"Tell me, Lilly, isn't Charlie just the most terrific nephew I could ever hope for?" Aunt Margaret pinched Charlie's cheek.

"I'm so lucky. He and Benny are such nice boys. Of course, having nieces would be wonderful, too. Tell me something, Lilly. Do you like dolls?"

"Dolls?" Lilly asked.

Charlie moved over slightly and stood behind Aunt Margaret, vigorously shaking his head. "No," he mouthed. "Say no." His mouth made a perfect O.

"Well, I can't say I'm interested in them anymore," Lilly said. "I mean, I liked them when I was little, but—"

"I'm talking about collecting dolls, of course. I've got this simply remarkable collection. In fact, I go to a lot of collectors' conventions, and I'm very active in the doll community." Aunt Margaret smiled. "Some people even consider me an expert."

"Wow," Lilly said, trying to sound enthused.

"You know what, Aunt Margaret? Lilly and I were just on our way to the dance floor when you stopped us," Charlie said, suddenly taking Lilly's arm in his. "And I'd hate for us not to be able to dance to one of Lilly's favorite songs."

"Oh, my. I had no idea! Yes, you two go right ahead and don't let me intrude on your special afternoon another minute. Shoo, shoo." Aunt Margaret gestured toward the dance floor. "And Lilly, we can talk more later, all right?"

"Sure thing," Lilly said, backing away. "Hey, nice escape move," she said to Charlie as they walked toward the dance floor, which was filled with young couples. A popular dance song was belting out of the speakers.

Charlie laughed. "You absolutely cannot get her started on that doll stuff. You'd die from boredom in less than three minutes—not that she'd limit herself to three minutes, of course. You'd be here for hours. Days, even. Standing in the same place, without food or water . . ."

"Oh, I'd find some way to get out of it," Lilly said. "Trust me." She and Charlie stepped onto the dance floor, made a small space for themselves, and started dancing. "Hey, how did you know this was one of my favorite songs?" Lilly asked over the loud drumbeat.

"You like *this?*" Charlie scoffed. "You've got to be kidding!"

"Why would I be kidding? This is a great song," she said. "Way better than that slow, twangy stuff *you* were listening to in the truck."

"I don't think so," Charlie replied, shuffling closer to her. "How can you even compare this kind of prepackaged, preprogrammed music to something as totally original as Crosby, Stills, and Nash?"

"That's what my father always says," Lilly complained. "I'm into music that came out in *this* decade."

Lilly had a feeling Charlie would get along great with her parents, who acted as if the sixties had never ended. The only problem was, he was sixteen and they were forty-six. Charlie wasn't a bad dancer, Lilly reflected, even if he didn't like the music or know any of the latest moves. He didn't look like a total fool, the way she would have expected. She couldn't believe she was actually having fun with him.

"Some nineties stuff is okay," Charlie said. "I

don't know. It's just one of those personal-taste things."

The song ended and the two of them stood there for a moment, waiting to see what the next one would be. Suddenly the slow, romantic strains of a love ballad from a new hit movie came wafting toward them. They each took an awkward step away from the other.

"Well, it's been fun," Lilly said. "But—"

"Wait a second," Charlie said. "Here comes Benny."

"So?" Lilly asked.

"Our bet—it's about having a date. A real date," Charlie said nervously.

"Oh, I get it. It's supposed to look like a date? Here, maybe this will help." Lilly put her hands on Charlie's shoulders and gazed up into his eyes. It was the least she could do, after he'd fixed up Sweetpea so well.

Charlie looked shocked as he put his hands on her waist. They moved slowly around the dance floor, swaying to the romantic music. Charlie pulled her a little closer as they squeezed past another couple. And Lilly didn't push him away. She looked up at him, and he smiled. She was getting carried away with the sexy music and felt a nearly irresistible urge to kiss him. What was happening to her?

The song ended, and Lilly just stood there with her arms around Charlie. *Wait a second,* she thought. *What are you doing?*

She stepped back. "Ah . . . I think I need to sit down," she said, at the same time as Charlie said, "I never did get anything to eat." They both laughed nervously.

As they walked off the dance floor Charlie called to someone sitting at a table. "I have to say hi to my cousin Rachel," he told Lilly. "I'll meet you at the buffet, okay?" He hurried off and Lilly stood motionless for a moment, watching Charlie hug his cousin. She wished he'd offered to introduce her.

Why would he? she told herself. *It's not as if this is a real date.* Still, it had almost started to feel like one when they were dancing. *Boy, this wedding stuff is really getting to me.* Lilly shook her head and made her way over toward the buffet table, where Benny and Sheila were standing in line.

"Charlie's some date, huh? Leaving you alone while he talks to Rachel," Benny said when Lilly caught up with them. "But don't worry, *we* won't leave you all by yourself. This is Sheila, by the way."

"Hi," Lilly said, "it's nice to meet you." She smiled at Sheila, wondering if she was in the same boat. Had Benny fixed *her* car? Was this how the swinging Roark cousins found dates in this town?

The thought made her smile as she picked up a plate and followed Benny and Sheila through the buffet line. She took a croissant, some sliced turkey

70

breast, and a side dish of pasta salad. She had almost reached the end of the line when one of the caterers slipped a fresh tray of tiny egg rolls into the warmer in front of her.

"Would you care for one, ma'am . . . Lilly?" the waiter asked.

Lilly's plate teetered in her hands. "*Bryan?* What are you doing here?"

Chapter Eight

"DIDN'T YOU KNOW I work for a catering company?" Bryan looked down at his fancy ruffled white shirt and black jacket. "These clothes kill me, but the money's not bad."

"Oh, yeah, right." Lilly nodded slowly, the horror of what had just happened—and was still happening—sinking in. "You work for a caterer. Right."

"Yeah. So what are you doing here?" Bryan asked.

Don't ask me that. Please don't ask me that, Lilly silently begged.

"I thought you'd be at the ball game with everyone else," Bryan continued, adjusting the tray in the warmer.

"So did I," Lilly said under her breath.

"What did you say?"

"Oh, just that . . . I thought I'd be there, too,"

Lilly said. "But then my, uh, my parents told me at the last minute that I had to come here. One of those family deals."

"So you're related to the bride and groom?" Bryan asked.

"Oh, no!" Lilly set down her plate on the table, horrified. Benny gave her a strange look and she turned away from him. "Nothing like that. It's . . . well, my dad works with the father of the . . . groom. Or his friend. Or something like that. *I* don't know," Lilly went on. "But for some reason we all had to come."

"So where's the rest of your family?" Bryan asked.

Lilly waved her fork in the air. "They're around somewhere. It's just me and my parents—and I had to get away from their table and . . . have something to eat." She looked down at the food on her plate, which suddenly seemed like a huge amount. She was making a pig of herself in front of Bryan. How embarrassing.

"Sounds like a pretty lame way to spend the afternoon," Bryan commented. "Hanging out with your parents, I mean."

You have no idea, Lilly thought, managing a small smile.

"Well, I should go back to the kitchen," Bryan said. "I'll see you around."

"Right," Lilly said. "Maybe later we could—"

"I'm back!" Charlie interrupted, touching Lilly's arm. "Sorry I had to leave you by yourself. So, how's the food look? What's good?"

Lilly turned slowly toward Charlie, restraining the urge to kick him in the shins. He was smiling at her, looking all friendly and happy to see her. She couldn't believe that less than five minutes earlier she'd actually wanted to kiss him. Charlie didn't even like her, she reminded herself; he was only going out with her to win a bet. And now this bet was ruining her life—and her chances with Bryan!

"So, would this be your dad?" Bryan asked Lilly, giving her a skeptical look. "You did say you were here with your parents."

"Did I?" Lilly replied, flustered. She tried to sound casual, but it didn't seem to be working. "Well, uh . . ."

"I'm Charlie, her *date*," Charlie interrupted. "Don't I know you from school?"

"I'm Bryan. So, Lilly, are you having a good time?" Bryan asked.

I was, she thought. *But now I'm miserable.* She didn't even know why she'd let herself have any fun in the first place. "It's okay," she said, shrugging.

"Well, I'd better get back to work," Bryan said.

Lilly smiled at him. "See you Monday, okay?" She wished there were some way she could let Bryan know she wasn't on a *real* date with Charlie. But he was gone before she could even begin to explain everything.

"So, did you miss me?" Charlie asked, dumping a large spoonful of fruit salad on his plate.

Lilly glared at him. "Like you wouldn't believe." She thought of a poster she'd seen in the window of

74

a travel agency once: *How Can I Miss You If You Won't Go Away?*

"So now what do we do?" Benny asked Charlie at the end of the afternoon.

Charlie shrugged. "Beats me. I guess we're going to have to come up with another bet."

"I know that, but what can it be? Since we've both proven we can get dates."

One way or the other, Charlie thought.

"Benny? I have to get going." Sheila had come up behind Benny and tapped him on the shoulder. "So, when do I get my tick—"

"C'mon, I'll give you a ride home," Benny said.

"Okay, fine, but when are you going to give me the—"

"We'll see you later!" Benny said cheerfully.

Charlie grabbed his arm. "Not so fast. What's Sheila talking about?"

"She really has to get going, don't you, Sheila?" Benny hustled her toward the car. "I'll talk to you later, Charlie. Nice meeting you, Lilly!" he called over his shoulder.

Charlie jogged after them. "You know, Benny, you never told me exactly how you got this date," he said in a low voice. "Care to divulge any of your secrets?"

"Sorry, man—we're late." Benny unlocked the passenger's-side door.

"Well, what are we going to do about the bet?" Charlie asked, following Benny around the car.

"How about double or nothing?" Benny asked.

"Huh?" Charlie asked. "What do you mean?"

"This was date one. Let's see if you can get date two with Lilly," Benny challenged. "What do you say?"

"Fine. No problem. We were probably going to go on another date soon, anyway."

"Really? That's funny; you guys didn't seem to be getting along that well. I mean, you have nothing in common. And no offense, but she's beautiful," Benny said.

"What's your point?" Charlie asked. "And didn't you see us dancing together?"

"For one dance, sure. But if I can't get another date with Sheila, I'll go on that cruise with Aunt Margaret," Benny said. "And if you can't get another date with Lilly, then you'll have to go."

Charlie thought it over for a minute. He didn't know how he'd convince Lilly to go out with him again. It might take a major miracle. But Benny seemed to have promised Sheila something for their date—he thought he'd heard her say something about tickets—so maybe Benny wouldn't be able to get another date with her, either.

"Auntie M.'s invited the two of us to her house for a barbecue next Saturday. Let's make that the date. That way we can both make sure it's all legit," Benny said.

"Okay, it's a deal," Charlie said.

"Cool. I'll talk to you tomorrow," Benny said as he got into the car. "Good luck."

"I won't need it, but thanks," Charlie said. He

watched Benny and Sheila drive off, then glanced back at the lawn, where Lilly was waiting for him, her arms folded across her chest. Pushing her long dark brown hair back over her shoulders, she looked completely irritated.

There was only one thing left to do, Charlie knew: start bargaining. And praying. How could he ask Lilly to go out with him again? She'd held up her end of their deal. Then a plan formed in his head. He'd spent about twelve hours working on her father's car and she'd spent only four hours with him so far, so didn't she owe him at least another four?

"Yeah. And pigs might fly." Lilly started laughing. "Has anyone ever told you that you have a really weird sense of humor, Charlie Roark?" She couldn't believe he wanted another date with her. No way. She had her own life to get on with, and it didn't include Charlie—especially since he'd ruined her chances with Bryan Bassani. "Look, it's been fun and all, but I really don't think we'll be going out again," she told him. "Thanks for fixing the car, though. So can we take off now?" She started walking toward the driveway, but Charlie didn't move.

Oh, no, she thought, *not this again.* She couldn't count the number of times she'd gone out with a guy once, only to find him getting all sappy when she'd tried politely to say good-bye. "What are you waiting for?" Lilly asked.

"Nothing, really. It's just that I keep forgetting

to ask you this. I mean, I figure no news is good news, but has your dad noticed anything different about the car yet?" Charlie asked.

Lilly hesitated.

"Well, has he?"

"No."

"Then I think you might just owe me another date," Charlie said calmly.

"What is this, blackmail?" Lilly demanded.

"It's called logic," Charlie said. "Maybe you've heard of it? *L-O-G-I-C?*"

"And my logic is *N-O*," Lilly retorted. "I don't see how I would possibly owe you another date, unless of course you're planning on fixing the car again. Because as far as I can figure, I kept my end of the bargain."

"Just listen to me for a second," Charlie pleaded. "It's about the bet. I need another date with you in order to win. Please. It's really important." He looked genuinely desperate.

Lilly sighed loudly. "Maybe, *maybe* I'll help you, if you'll tell me what this bet is all about."

Out of the corner of her eye she saw a large purple and orange blur approaching. "Kids! Don't leave before I can take your picture!" Aunt Margaret hurried over to them, a large camera swinging around her neck.

Charlie looked at Lilly, a pained expression on his face. She just shook her head and stared at the ground. Lilly didn't feel like being nice to anybody. All she wanted was to go home, take a shower, change, and go out with her friends. Not that the afternoon had been terrible—it had actually been fun, at least until she ran into Bryan at the buffet table.

"Oh, Lilly and Charlie, I'd just be devastated if I didn't get a picture of you two, looking so nice and all dressed up," Aunt Margaret gushed. "Why don't you stand over there by that lovely tree?" She took Lilly's hand. "Did you have a nice time, dear?"

"Unbelievable," Lilly muttered. "Unbelievably nice, I mean." She smiled at Charlie's aunt.

"Okay, you two. Get closer," Aunt Margaret instructed. "Closer." She waited a moment. Charlie and Lilly were standing on opposite sides of the tree trunk. "Come on, Charlie. Go over there and put your arm around her," Aunt Margaret urged.

Charlie took a few steps toward Lilly. She moved closer to him, figuring if she didn't go ahead and get it over with, she might be standing under that tree all night while Aunt Margaret waited for a perfect photo opportunity.

"Now put your arms around each other," Aunt Margaret instructed, "and kiss for the camera."

"Aunt Margaret, we're not the ones who got married today," Charlie said. "I think you've gotten us confused with Jack and Lorraine. Nobody wants our picture."

"Kids, trust me—you'll want to remember this day."

Trust me—we won't! Lilly thought, glancing at Charlie. But she had a feeling that if she wanted to leave, she was going to have to give in to Aunt Margaret's request.

Charlie gingerly put his arm around her shoulders. "It's only for a second," he muttered. "Just humor her for my sake, please?"

"Now let's see a big kiss for the camera," Aunt Margaret prompted.

Lilly looked at Charlie out of the corner of her eye. He was looking at her the same way, and she almost laughed out loud. "We're a pathetic excuse for a date, aren't we?" she said.

Charlie pulled her closer to him. "I know one of your rules said no kissing, but in this case we're going to have make an exception."

Lilly wasn't sure whether she wanted to kiss him or not. While they were dancing earlier, nothing would have made her happier than to kiss Charlie as he held her tight. And now that they were so close to each other again, she'd forgotten why they'd been fighting less than ten minutes earlier. Right then all she could concentrate on were his deep blue eyes and the way they were looking at her. "Rules are made to be broken, right?" Lilly said.

Charlie leaned closer, and she stretched on her tiptoes to meet his lips in a kiss. Her mouth brushed against his and the moment was very special . . . until Aunt Margaret cried out, "Perfect! Got it!"

Charlie's arm was off Lilly's shoulders before she could even stop smiling for the camera. She wondered what that was all about. Hadn't he enjoyed being so close to her? It sure had seemed as though he'd wanted to kiss her.

"I'll get double prints. Now, I assume Charlie's told you all about the barbecue at my house next weekend," Aunt Margaret said. "I'll look forward to chatting with you more then, Lilly."

"Barbecue?" Lilly mumbled, still stunned from what had just happened, or almost happened, between her and Charlie. His reaction to their near-miss kiss was confusing her. Just as they'd been about to really kiss, he'd backed off. Was it because his aunt had interrupted them? Was he looking for an excuse to get out of it quickly? How dare he! He should consider himself lucky that Lilly even allowed him to kiss her on the cheek!

"Oh, now, Charlie's always waiting till the last minute for these things, but trust me, you're invited. We'll see you there. Take care!" Aunt Margaret left to take pictures of other departing guests.

Lilly turned to Charlie. "Is that why I have to go out with you again—because of Aunt Margaret's barbecue?"

"Not exactly," Charlie said, looking a little sheepish. "You asked about the bet. Well, you know it was about bringing a date to the wedding. Only Benny brought one, too, so we're even. And now we have to up the bet. That's why I need another date."

"Maybe you should ask someone else," Lilly said. She was tired of feeling like a poker chip in a casino. And she sure didn't appreciate being tossed aside after that kiss, even if it was only for the camera. She'd felt something for Charlie—otherwise she would never have kissed him, bet or no bet—but apparently it was all an act to him.

"Let's talk about it in the car," Charlie said.

"You mean tow truck," Lilly corrected.

"Right." Charlie smiled sheepishly. They walked over to the truck and climbed in, and Charlie started the engine. He slowly pulled out of the driveway onto the road.

"So this bet—well, I can't bring anyone else. It has to be you," Charlie said. "And the reason we made this bet in the first place isn't anything sleazy, I swear. You see, Benny and I don't want to go on a vacation with Aunt Margaret—it's this cruise to Alaska she's all excited about. And the loser of this bet has to go with her. You have to help me win."

"A cruise to Alaska? A cruise? Oh, that's real life-or-death material," Lilly said.

"Can you imagine spending a week with her? I'd go crazy," Charlie said.

"What about her? You think she wouldn't go crazy spending a week with *you?*" Lilly asked.

"Come on, Lilly, you have to admit it'd be misery. You've talked to her—you know what it would be like!" Charlie cried.

"No. What I know is, you're going to have to find some other way to get out of your little iceberg vacation," Lilly said. "Count me out!" She didn't feel like spending another afternoon performing fake dances and kisses for an audience.

"And what I know is, if your father gets a bill from Roark's Auto Body on Tuesday, you're going to be stuck in the house for the rest of your life," Charlie replied.

"Oh, nice! Now you're threatening me."

"No!" Charlie swerved around a corner, going too fast. "I'm just saying I did a ton of work on your car—your dad's car, I mean—and the least you could do is help me out just a little more."

"I already went to the wedding with you, danced with you, *kissed* you—"

"Barely," Charlie interrupted.

Lilly glared at him. He didn't know the first thing about kissing! "You know what? I'm starting to wish you'd junked that car instead of fixing it!"

"I wish I did too—with you in it!" Charlie retorted as he pulled the truck over in front of her house.

Lilly flung the door open and hopped out onto the pavement, almost spraining her ankle as she landed. "Make up your mind, Charlie—do you want me dead, or do you want another date?"

She slammed the door closed and Charlie took off, the truck's tires squealing as he peeled around the corner at the end of the block.

"Good riddance!" she yelled after him.

Chapter Nine

LILLY WOKE UP Sunday morning feeling completely refreshed. She lazily got out of bed, pulling back the curtains to find a beautiful sunny day. She hoped it was as warm outside as it looked. She loved spring.

The previous night had been so much fun. Lilly and six of her friends had gone out for pizza, then to a late movie. She couldn't remember the last time she'd laughed so hard.

It was almost good enough to make me forget about my strange encounter with Charlie Roark, she thought. Now it all came back to her: Aunt Margaret with her camera; Bryan at the buffet table; Charlie being rude, kissing her, and then asking for another date. Lilly couldn't believe she'd kissed Charlie. She hated to admit that she'd actually enjoyed it—even if it was just a quick peck on the lips, and even if he had acted afterward as if nothing had happened.

And now there was no way she could get out of going to Aunt Margaret's barbecue with him the next weekend. Charlie had an unfair advantage over her. And, she supposed, he was right—maybe she did owe him more than one date for all the work he'd done on Sweetpea. But two Saturdays in a row? Lilly was afraid people might forget about her if she missed any more weekend social activities. Maybe she could barter with Charlie, turn it into a short breakfast date. Coffee and donuts.

Lilly pulled a robe over her pajamas and headed downstairs for breakfast, where she found her father sitting alone at the kitchen table. "Where's Mom?" Lilly asked, sitting down across from him.

"She left early to get in some work at her office," Mr. Cameron said. "You know how she is about Sunday mornings."

Lilly poured herself a bowl of cereal. Her mother was famous for working all the hours that other people normally relaxed in. It wasn't that she worked all the time—just during odd times. She always said she could concentrate better then. "So what have you been up to?" Lilly asked.

Her father wiped a drop of coffee off the wood table. "I was puttering around in the garage a little bit. And then I decided to wash the car." He paused.

Lilly felt a cornflake stick to the back of her throat. "Mm-hm," she said, glancing nervously at him.

"And as I was washing it, something occurred to me," he continued. "Something I want to talk to you about."

Oh, no. Here it comes. Lilly forced herself to sound casual. "About what?" she asked.

"It's kind of serious. Are you sure you're awake yet?" Mr. Cameron fiddled with the loaf of bread by the toaster, rearranging the stack of napkins beside it.

He's so mad he can't even look at me, Lilly thought with a shudder. *He's going to tell me that I've completely let him down, that all his trust in me has been shattered. And I deserve everything he says.* "Yeah, I'm awake," Lilly said. "What is it?"

"It's about the car." He turned and faced her, his expression stern.

The spoon in Lilly's hand started wobbling. She was so nervous, she could barely breathe. That stupid Charlie Roark. He sure wasn't going to get another date with her now. In fact, he was going to owe her big time. Maybe he could visit her in solitary confinement. "What about the car?"

"I want to go over the rules. As you know, now that you have your license you're allowed to use the cars, but you need to ask our permission each time. Right?"

"Right," Lilly said slowly.

"And that's because we've needed some time to get used to the idea of you driving alone. Because we wanted you to learn that this is a privilege, not a right," her father continued. "Are we clear on that?"

Lilly nodded. "Clear as . . . well, clear," she said. *Clear as my social schedule's going to be, once I'm grounded for life.*

"Good. Well, all that's about to change," Mr. Cameron said, emphasizing his point by twisting the lid back onto the jar of blueberry jam on the table and sliding it over to Lilly.

She stopped the jar just before it crashed into her cereal bowl and looked at her father. She wished he would just get to the point already. She couldn't take this long, drawn-out torture anymore. "Look, Dad, I know I made a big mis—" she began.

"Your mother and I would like to make you an offer," Mr. Cameron said at the same time.

"Go ahead," Lilly said.

"No, you can speak," he said.

"No, you go first," she insisted. *I almost blew the whole thing!*

"You're going to need a car for your job this summer," he began. "The country club is a good five miles from here, and I don't want you riding your bike home late at night."

"Uh-huh," Lilly said slowly.

"So here's our proposal. The three of us will sit down and work out a budget. You agree to put in half of your summer earnings, and we'll put in the rest you need to get a used car. Nothing expensive, just something functional. It may not look good, but it'll do the job and the insurance payments will be lower that way."

Lilly had a vague sense that her father had

stopped talking and was waiting for her response, but she was too stunned to do anything except just stare at him. Was he offering to help her buy a car—after what she'd done? Was this really happening?

"Lilly? You look upset. I know you'd rather have a new convertible, but this is just your first car. They'll get better," her father promised. "You're going to have a car this summer, and for your senior year. Isn't that *good* news?"

Lilly shook her head, trying to snap out of it. "Dad, that's *great* news!" she finally said. "It's just . . . I never expected this. It's such a surprise."

"Really? You were expecting a BMW?" Her father smiled.

"No!" Lilly cried. "I wasn't expecting anything. This is really terrific of you guys. I'm overwhelmed, that's all."

This was fantastic news! She would have her own car in two months. Maybe even less than that. No more begging for rides, no more biking to the mall . . . Charlie had told her that his father owned a used-car lot, adjacent to his garage. Maybe if she was a little nicer to him, she'd get a good deal on a car she'd actually like!

"Well, we think you've proved you can handle the responsibility," Mr. Cameron said. "And we're counting on you to keep that up."

"Oh, I will," Lilly promised. "You can trust me." *Most of the time, anyway.*

★　　★　　★

"Your parents are giving you a car?" Tracy laughed. "Is that ironic or what?"

"It's more than ironic, it's excellent," Lilly said excitedly. "Can you believe it?"

She and Tracy were on their way to a school newspaper staff meeting Monday afternoon. Lilly had begun working for the paper a few weeks earlier with the hope she might be made an editor for her senior year. Writing wasn't one of her best skills, but she worked on the school's activities page, which usually meant a lot of short pieces about upcoming events. She left the serious writing to the other people on staff.

"Not really, no. I always knew you were lucky, but this is verging on the ridiculous," Tracy said as she opened the door to the newspaper office. "When you add it to the bad luck of having to go out with Charlie Roark, though, it kind of evens out."

"Shh," Lilly warned her. "You promised to keep that a secret."

"Lilly, just the person I need to talk to," Jem Matthews interrupted. Jem, the features editor at the paper, looked like a typical newspaper writer— tiny, oval wire-rimmed glasses, hair that was always messy, never wearing anything but oxford shirts and jeans.

"Really? What's up?" Lilly asked, going over to Jem's desk.

"There's an event I want you to write a preview article about," he said, shuffling some papers around on his desk. "I need you to do it today, though, so we can get it in this week's issue."

"Sure," Lilly said. "No problem. What's the event?"

"You know how there's an auto club here, right?" Jem asked.

"There is?" Lilly had never heard of it before.

"Yeah. It's got about ten students in it and Mr. McDuff's the advisor. Anyway, they're doing a fund-raiser on Sunday and I want to give them a lot of publicity," Jem explained.

Lilly took a small notepad out of her book bag and grabbed a pen out of the cup on Jem's desk. "Give me the details."

Jem consulted a sheet of paper. "It's a car wash they're sponsoring over at the old fire station on Monroe. And the proceeds are going toward MS research."

"MS. Multiple sclerosis?" Lilly asked.

Jem nodded. "Yeah. So do you think you can write something and get it to me first thing tomorrow?"

"Sure. I'll just go by Mr. McDuff's office after our meeting and talk to him about it," Lilly said. "Thanks for the assignment." The more assignments she got and did well, the better her chances of winning an editorial position the next year.

"Actually, it says here you should talk to the organizer of the event. That's . . ." Jem skimmed the paper. "Charlie Roark."

Lilly stared at Jem. "What did you just say?"

"You need to talk to Charlie Roark. It says you can find him at the auto club—you know, over by auto shop—this afternoon. I just got this today," Jem explained. "Okay, Lilly?"

Charlie Roark, organizing a fund-raiser that was connected to school somehow? *That doesn't sound like him,* Lilly thought. She was beginning to wonder what else she didn't know about Charlie. Maybe if she knew more about him, she'd get along with him better.

Get real, she told herself. *After this interview and the barbecue Saturday, you won't even say hello to the guy, just like before.*

Charlie practically froze when he saw Lilly walking across the school garage's cement floor toward him. *What is she doing here?* he wondered. All day he'd dreaded seeing her, after the way they'd fought Saturday afternoon. He hated confrontations, but he wasn't about to apologize, either. Asking for another date was far from being unreasonable. But Lilly had acted as if she'd rather go skydiving without a parachute than spend another second with him.

What made him even more uncomfortable than their argument was that kiss. He'd been glad Aunt Margaret had interrupted them. Kiss Lilly Cameron? He'd barely even kissed *any* girl before, not since summer camp, anyway, when he was twelve. And he'd been so nervous, afraid he wouldn't kiss Lilly right, that he'd backed off as soon as he got the chance. He could just imagine how much she'd tease him if he turned out to be a bad kisser.

Lilly came closer, and Charlie pretended to

straighten the toolbox on the table. He felt over-whelmingly shy all of a sudden.

"Charlie?" she said softly, sounding tentative.

He turned around, leaned back against the counter, and nervously wiped his hands on a rag. "Hi," he said.

"Hi." Lilly smiled and took a look around the garage. "So this is where you hang out, huh?"

Charlie shrugged. "Some of the time. Monday and Wednesday afternoons." Lilly was being so nice and friendly, but he wasn't sure whether he trusted her or not. Seeing her again wasn't as hard as he'd feared. It felt like the calm feeling outdoors after a big thunderstorm, when the wind stopped blowing and birds began chirping again.

"Charlie, I have to hand it to you again," Lilly said. "My dad's washed, waxed, and practically slept in his car, and he hasn't noticed a thing."

"Good," Charlie said. "I'm glad."

"Me too. You don't know *how* glad. My parents are actually going to help me buy a used car in a couple of months or so. I'm totally in the clear, thanks to you. So I've decided I owe you another date." Lilly shrugged. "That is, if you still want one."

Charlie grinned. "Definitely! I was just standing here picturing myself aboard the ship, playing shuf-fleboard on deck with a bunch of old ladies."

"Good. So you'll pick me up Saturday and we'll go to Aunt Margaret's barbecue?" Lilly asked.

"What about your new car?" Charlie asked.

"Oh, I won't be getting that for a while," Lilly said. "Probably not until the beginning of the summer. But maybe I can buy it at your father's used-car lot—think you can get me a good deal?"

"No problem. We have special deals for wedding dates. I wish I had my own car."

"You don't have a car?" Lilly asked.

"No. Why would I?" Charlie said.

"I don't know. I just assumed that since your dad fixes cars, maybe you have a bunch of them around the garage," Lilly said.

"Well, it's our policy to *return* the cars after we fix them," Charlie said.

Lilly laughed. "No, I know that! I just figured if somebody forgot to pick up their car, you might get to keep it."

"No such luck," Charlie said. "You know what I really want? A car like your dad's. That thing is so cool. I loved driving it, even if it was only a couple of miles back to your house."

"Yeah, me too. Whatever I get isn't going to be anything special," Lilly said. "But it'll get me where I need to go."

Charlie resisted the urge to say, *Not if you keep driving the way you do.* But since she was making the effort to be nice and civil, he would too.

"Anyway, I was looking for you for two reasons," Lilly went on. "First, to tell you I could go on Saturday, and second, because I work for the *Herald* and we're doing a story on your car wash this weekend. I was told to talk to you."

"You work for the *Herald?*" Charlie asked.

"Yeah. Why do you sound so surprised?" Lilly asked. "I mean, I know I'm not brilliant in English class, but—"

"No, I didn't mean it that way," Charlie quickly explained. "It's just—what *don't* you do around here? You run the student council, you're on the cheerleading and pep squads, you write for the paper, you know half the people in this school—"

"Two-thirds, actually," Lilly interrupted with a smile.

"Okay, two-thirds. I doubt if I know more than ten people, total. Next you're going to tell me you play sports all three seasons, and you're secretly the president of the backgammon club. You aren't, are you?" Charlie asked.

"No. Actually, it's the French club. And I'm only the secretary," Lilly said.

"*C'est dommage,*" Charlie said.

"You speak French? Wow, I didn't know that," Lilly said. "How come I never see you in class?"

"There *is* more than one section, Lilly," Charlie pointed out, shaking his head. *The Mega-Ego is back.* He wasn't surprised Lilly thought the only section that existed was the one she was in.

"Right. Okay, let's get down to business." She brushed off a metal stool and sat down, pulling a pink notebook out of her book bag.

It was hard for Charlie to take seriously anyone who carried around a pink notebook. He watched her jot down a few notes at the top of the page, and noticed that the polish on her fingernails matched the color of the notebook. He'd never known anyone so coordinated before. He glanced down at his unlaced sneakers and the frayed bottom hem of his faded denim overalls. No, they definitely had nothing in common.

"Tell me about the car wash," Lilly prompted. "It's to raise money for MS research?"

Charlie nodded. "Right." He gave Lilly all the details of the event, and she wrote them down. "Can you give us a big article? I want to make sure lots of people come."

"I'll try," Lilly said, "but I don't have that much pull. Maybe if you tell me more, I can stretch it into a longer article. For instance, whose idea was this?"

"Mine," Charlie said.

"And why MS in particular? Why not some other cause or charity?" Lilly said.

Charlie wasn't sure he should confide in Lilly. He felt he could trust her, though. "My mother has MS. Ever since she was diagnosed, I've become aware of what a horrible disease it is and how many people have it."

Lilly didn't say anything right away. She didn't write anything down, either. "Wow, Charlie. I had no idea."

"Yeah. Actually, that's why I was late to pick you up for the wedding," he explained. "My mom's been having a lot of trouble with her balance, and she was pretty upset that day. She was walking down the hall all dressed up for the wedding and she suddenly fell. It sounds like a little thing, but Mom knows it's only going to get worse. She gets pretty down sometimes. Well, anyway, that's why she didn't come to the wedding."

"I can't imagine what that would be like," Lilly said. "It must be hard on your dad . . . and you too. Really hard."

Charlie hadn't expected such a sympathetic response. He cleared his throat. "So do you think you have enough to go on?" he asked. "If you want, I can help you write the article. It would take me only a couple of minutes to put it all together for you."

Lilly stood up, closed her notebook, and jammed it into her book bag. "I think I can write my own article, thank you very much. It might take me a couple of hours instead of a couple of minutes, because I'm not a genius like you. I may only get B's on my essays instead of getting them handed around to the rest of the class to read, but I *think* I can handle it."

"Lilly, I didn't mean you couldn't," Charlie protested. "I just thought maybe I—"

"I heard what you said, and I know what you meant. You don't think I'll do a good job," Lilly accused. "Well, I will, okay? And tons of people will come to the car wash. I'll even tell my parents to come, because I think it's important. But don't stand there and tell me how you should write the article instead."

"A little touchy today, aren't we?" Charlie asked.

All he'd wanted to do was help—what was so wrong with that?

"No, a little insulting and rude, actually." Lilly turned and walked out of the garage.

"I'll see you Saturday, right?" Charlie called after her. "Lilly?"

Chapter Ten

"**W**HERE'S THE TRUCK?" Lilly asked as she climbed into the green minivan and sat down. "I don't know if I can handle this clean seat. Whose car is this, anyway?"

"Sorry. It's Aunt Margaret's. I hate driving this almost as much as you probably miss the tow truck," Charlie said.

"Is that possible?" Lilly teased.

"I'm serious. I hate minivans," Charlie said. "I'm making a pledge right here and now that I will never own one, never be friends with anyone who owns one, never—"

"Wait a second. Are you saying that if my new car turns out to be a minivan, you're going to abandon me—just like that?" Lilly snapped her fingers.

"Without a doubt. You'd be history."

Lilly smiled. A week earlier she would have

been thrilled to have that information: get a minivan, get rid of Charlie. Now she just found it amusing. She knew she ought to be mad at him for the way he'd acted like such a know-it-all in the school garage, but it didn't seem like such a big deal now. She'd decided to make the best of her afternoon with Charlie. As soon as he dropped her off that night, their deal would be officially over. "You've got standards, don't you? No Fruity Fun Drink, no nineties music, no minivans . . ."

"Hey, I have principles like you wouldn't believe," Charlie said. "What about you? Are there any rules you live by?"

Lilly drummed her fingers on the armrest. "I'm not sure I could list them, I have so many."

"Give it a try. Toss out your top ten," he said.

They were driving past the town golf course, and Lilly watched as a woman tried to chip her ball out of a sand trap beside the road. "Since you mentioned food, music, and cars, I'll stick to those. Number one, no tofu hot dogs—"

"Oh, come on—those are great. Have you ever tried one?" Charlie asked.

"My mom's on this midlife health-food kick, and we had them last weekend, for your information." Lilly made a face. "And I'm *still* getting over it. Second, you'll never catch me listening to folk music, and third . . . Well, I was going to say no huge cars that are bigger than my bedroom, but I think I'm going to have to go with the no-minivan rule."

"All right! Congratulations, lucky contestant, you've won an all-expenses-paid trip to—"

"Alaska!" Lilly interrupted with a smile.

Charlie turned to her. "That's not funny, okay?"

"Oh, relax already. As of today, you'll be off the hook. Tell me the truth—wouldn't you like to see Alaska someday? I bet it's really beautiful," Lilly said.

"I've got a great idea. You go with Auntie M.," Charlie said. "Why didn't I think of it before? It's the perfect solution."

"Charlie, stop dreaming, okay? I already have plans for my summer vacation," Lilly told him. "And I hardly even know your crazy aunt."

"You will after today," Charlie said. "You'll know *all* about her—and her doll collection." He pulled into the driveway at Aunt Margaret's house.

"This looks familiar," Lilly said as she got out of the van. "Uh . . . Lilly?" Charlie lingered by the van, while Lilly had started heading for the house. "There's something I just want to, you know, run by you."

Lilly walked back toward him, suddenly feeling nervous. Why did Charlie sound so serious? "Okay," she said. "What?"

"This bet between Benny and me. Just getting you to come to this barbecue wasn't enough," he began. "In order to prove we're really dating, it has to seem like you really . . ."

"Like I like you?" Lilly asked. "No, wait—that's probably not enough. You want it to seem like I love you, like I'm *in* love with you, don't you?"

"You don't have to go overboard!" Charlie said, blushing. "Just be nice to me. Because if I don't win this bet, I'm going to *jump* overboard, and that's the last anyone's ever going to see of me."

"Until your rope bracelets wash up on shore," Lilly teased. "Okay, let me get this straight. If I'm not affectionate toward you, you'll off yourself? Gee, Charlie, I didn't know you cared." She smiled.

Charlie laughed. "Give me a break, okay? Just pretend you like me. You know, as if we're more than just friends."

"Exactly what are you expecting, Charlie?" Lilly asked. "Would you like me to give you a big, fat kiss right in front of your cousin? Sorry, but that's against my rules, remember? I'd love to oblige, but what can I do? My hands are tied."

"C'mon, think of it as a game. And once we fool Benny, the whole thing's over. Hey, I'll even buy you a hot-fudge sundae for your troubles."

Lilly stared at him. "How did you know I like hot fudge?"

"Doesn't everyone? I know you hang out at Sandy's, and they make the best hot-fudge sundaes around here," Charlie said. "So what do you say? Do you think you can pretend to genuinely like me for the next couple of hours?"

"Don't worry, Charlie—I won't let you down," Lilly said teasingly. They walked toward the house, and her stomach growled as she detected the aroma of grilling meat. "But I'll tell you one thing. If those are tofu hot dogs I smell cooking, I'm out of here."

*   *   *

Charlie leaned back in his chair, propping his feet on the deck railing. He smiled as Lilly came outside onto the deck. "Didn't think you'd ever get out of there, did you?" Charlie asked her.

"Half an hour," Lilly grumbled. "I was in there half an hour! Thanks for rescuing me."

Charlie tilted his head toward Benny and Sheila, who were sitting at the same table, watching her.

A broad smile flashed across Lilly's face. "While I'm up, would you like me to get you some more of those delicious baked beans . . . Sweetpea?" She put her hand on Charlie's shoulder.

Charlie tried not to laugh, especially when she used the nickname of her father's car. If Benny only knew. "Thanks, but I'm full," he told her. He knew she would have killed him if he'd actually asked her to get him anything.

"Why haven't you asked *me* if I want seconds?" Benny asked Sheila.

Sheila looked as if she were about to punch Benny. But then she said, smiling, "I'm sorry, I guess I just forgot. Can I get you anything?"

"Yeah. How about another burger, and put lots of ketchup and relish on it, okay?" Benny turned to Charlie, then apparently changed his mind. "Actually, Sheila, you don't need to wait on me. I can get it myself." He pushed back his chair and went inside.

Charlie couldn't believe how well the afternoon was going. He and Lilly weren't fighting, the food was great, and they were relaxed, sitting together on the deck. Charlie was determined to enjoy this day, since he had to work the next Saturday. The only problem was, Sheila and Benny seemed to be hitting it off, too. That meant he and Benny would have to come up with yet another way to resolve the question of who was going on that cruise.

"Have these boys told you about the exciting trip one of them will be taking with me in June?" Aunt Margaret asked Lilly and Sheila as she came outside with Benny and sat in a purple webbed chaise lounge on the deck.

"A little bit," Lilly said, trying not to laugh.

"Do you know that they haven't been able to decide which one of them will be the lucky one to come to Alaska with me?" Aunt Margaret shook her head and her orange-red hair didn't move. "Of course, it is the chance of a lifetime. I'm starting to think I should have gotten three tickets instead of two—then they wouldn't have to fight over it. Maybe it's not too late. I could call my travel agent and see if there's an extra berth available."

"No!" Benny said, dropping his hamburger onto his plate.

Aunt Margaret stared at him.

"What Benny means is, that's way too expensive," Charlie interrupted. "You're already doing enough. And what with spending so much for Jack's wedding and everything—"

"Actually, the Hansens picked up most of that,"

Aunt Margaret said. "We hosted the reception here only because it was a prettier spot."

"Still, I bet the rehearsal dinner put you back quite a bit," Charlie argued.

"Yeah," Benny finally piped up. "Besides, it'll be a lot more fun if it's just the two of us. We can hang out together—"

"But Benny sleeps until noon every day, so you wouldn't even see him for half the trip," Charlie said. "You'll have a lot more fun with me. Think of all the exploring we can do together. Benny would just sit on the deck working on his tan." He looked at his cousin, feeling superior. Aunt Margaret didn't need to know they were killing themselves to get *out* of going on this trip. Let her think they were fighting each other for the chance to go with her, instead of the opposite.

"Well, I'm sure you boys will find a fair way to decide who will be the lucky one," Aunt Margaret said.

"How about a duel?" Lilly suggested. "Whoever's still standing at the end gets to go."

Sheila cracked up. "A duel," she said in between giggles. "That's hilarious!"

Now Charlie knew for sure that Sheila didn't want to go out with Benny any more than Lilly wanted to be with him. Knowing that made him feel kind of low. Wasn't he a better catch than Benny?

"You have a very strange sense of humor, dear," Aunt Margaret said, looking at Lilly as if she were inspecting an odd exhibit at a school science fair.

Charlie was used to that look; he got it often from his aunt.

"She'd have to be strange, to go out with Charlie," Benny joked.

"Hey, let's not get personal," Charlie said. "I've had enough of sitting around. Who wants to play croquet?"

"I thought you only played games involving bouncing things off your knee," Lilly said. "You know, you should take up soccer."

"Didn't Charlie tell you? He used to play all the time," Benny said. "Until he hurt his knee. Now he can't play without pain."

"Oh. That's too bad," Lilly said.

Charlie knew Lilly had dated a couple of guys on the soccer team. Apparently, being on a team was some sort of requirement for her crowd. Too bad she didn't realize that not everybody could be on a team—and not everyone wanted to be. It wasn't a statement about a person's character, the way she seemed to think.

"Yeah, I miss playing," Charlie said. "But I've found other stuff I like to do. Stuff that's just as important."

Lilly seemed a bit taken aback by his tone. "Sure, if you call tossing a beanbag against a statue important."

Charlie was ready to get into an argument with her when he remembered the bet. Instead, he said, "Pumpkin, you have your school activities, and I have mine. You know we're different that way."

105

"Some of the greatest romances have been be-tween extremely different people," Aunt Margaret put in. "Scarlett and Rhett in *Gone With the Wind*, for example . . . and then there's *The Way We Were*, of course. Hubble and . . . what was her name?"

"So where do you keep the croquet set around here?" Lilly asked Charlie, interrupting Aunt Margaret's talk of romance. They walked around the yard placing wickets in the lawn, which was still slightly trampled from the reception the week before. Then they each chose a mallet. "You go first, Lilly," Charlie said. "Pumpkin."

"That's okay, Sweetpea, I'll go after you," Lilly said. She smiled at him.

"*Some*body play," Benny said, "before it gets dark."

Charlie made his first hit and sent the ball across the yard, where it stopped just inches from the first wicket.

"Not bad," Benny said.

Lilly went next. She slammed the ball so hard that it flew across the lawn and smacked right into Charlie's. He was surprised; he looked at the ball, then back at Lilly, then back at the ball.

"All right! Take your free hit!" Benny cheered.

"Way to go, Lilly!" Sheila said.

Charlie followed Lilly over to where their cro-quet balls were lying, just outside the first wicket. "Now, I can either take a free shot, or send your ball somewhere and then keep going, right?" Lilly asked.

"Uh-huh." Charlie nodded.

"Okay, then." Lilly put her foot on her own ball and smacked her mallet against it, sending Charlie's ball off under a bush at the edge of the lawn.

"Excellent!" Benny cried.

"How could you do that to me?" Charlie asked, putting on his hangdog expression for Lilly.

"Sorry, Charlie." Lilly laughed.

"It went into a huge gully over there—I'll never get it out," Charlie complained. Didn't she have any sympathy?

Lilly took a bow, then tapped her ball through the wicket and prepared to move on to the next.

"How did you do that?" Charlie asked, dumbfounded.

"I don't know why you're so surprised, unless of course you thought that a cheerleader couldn't play sports," Lilly said.

"I never said that. I'm sure cheerleading's demanding, in its own way."

"For your information, we train just as hard as any other team," Lilly said. "Our workouts are incredibly tough. I bet you couldn't keep up with us for fifteen minutes."

"Yeah, but do they involve croquet? You whaled on that thing like you were a pro."

"Oh, I used to be on the field hockey team in junior high." Lilly put the mallet on her shoulder. "Don't start to whine, Charlie. Why don't you let me help you with your next shot?" She followed him over to the gully where she'd shot his orange ball. Lilly put her arms around Charlie's waist, her hands over his, as he stepped up to the ball. "Hold the mallet like this," she coached.

Charlie looked over his shoulder at her. They hadn't been that close since they'd danced together at Jack's wedding . . . when he'd first felt the urge to kiss her.

Lilly rested her chin on his shoulder. "Think you can manage to hit it in the right direction?"

"Yeah, sure," Charlie said. "Just watch." He swung his mallet hard and his ball flew across the yard, smacking right into Benny's.

"No fair," Benny protested. "She helped."

"All right!" Charlie and Lilly gave each other a high five. Then, still holding onto his hand, Lilly pulled Charlie close and kissed him. Only this time it wasn't a little peck of a kiss, like the other day. Lilly pressed her soft lips against his as if she meant it, as if there was real passion behind it. This was a kiss with real intensity; it left Charlie tingling all over.

Then, before he could respond by kissing her back the way he wanted to, Lilly pulled away. "Nice shot," she said, winking at him. He stared into her eyes, wondering if she was just playing with him or if she'd really wanted to kiss him.

"All right, all right, let's just get back to the game already," Benny complained. "Hey, Charlie, are you going to send me into the bushes or what?"

Charlie wandered over to Benny, his head in a daze. Was that kiss for real? Charlie continued to wonder. Or was it just part of the plan to fool Benny? Did Lilly honestly like him?

You asked her to act nice toward you, and she's just going along with the plan, Charlie reminded himself. *Nothing more, nothing less.*

"I can't believe you guys *still* haven't settled your bet," Lilly told Charlie when he pulled the minivan up in front of her house later that afternoon. "Let's get one thing clear, Charlie. I will not continue to be part of your plan."

If it hadn't been for his stupid bet, Lilly wouldn't have been worrying about the way Charlie made her feel. It had been bad enough when they'd started to get along, but now they'd shared a *real* kiss—and Lilly had been the one who initiated it! Playing a game for Benny was one thing . . . but Lilly knew that deep down, she'd *wanted* to kiss Charlie.

Charlie Roark? She was obviously getting carried away with the dating charade, and it was time to put a stop to this game before anything else happened between them. Even if kissing Charlie had made Lilly feel as if she were floating.

"No, it won't involve you anymore," Charlie said. "I promise. We'll just have to come up with something else. Like maybe a croquet game—winner take all."

"I don't know," Lilly said. "Croquet might not be the best choice for you. The goal is *not* to go to Alaska, right?"

"Maybe you can give me a few more lessons. . . ." He seemed about to say something else, but he shook his head instead. "Well, I have to get this horrible minivan back to Aunt Margaret."

"Okay. Thanks for all the great food. I really had a nice time." Lilly opened the door and got out of the van.

"Lilly?" Charlie asked.

"Yeah?" She turned around and looked at him.

"I was just wondering if maybe sometime, you know, if you're not busy, we could—"

"Lilly! You're back. I'm not sure where you've been, but now you're back," Lilly's father said as he strode toward them from the side of the garage. He wiped his hands against his khaki pants, spreading dirt all over them.

"Hi, Dad," Lilly said. Why did parents always show up at the most awkward times? She knew Charlie was about to ask her out. And she wondered what her response would have been.

"I thought you were at the mall," Mr. Cameron said. "With Tracy and Kelly and the rest of the gang."

"I was," Lilly began.

"She was," Charlie said at the same time. They exchanged nervous glances. "And I offered to give her a ride home because . . . I was coming by this way on my way home. I hope that's okay," Charlie said.

"I'm Curtis Cameron." Lilly's father held out his hand.

"Charlie Roark." Charlie shook his hand.

Lilly thought she was going to die. Her father

was shaking hands with the guy who'd fixed Sweetpea, and he didn't know anything about it.

"Charlie, I know you've probably got to get home in a minute, but I wonder if you would help me with something," Mr. Cameron said.

"Dad, I'm sure I can help you with whatever it is," Lilly offered. She didn't want Charlie at her house any longer than he had to be. She had a bad feeling that if she stood there a second longer with Charlie and her father, the guilt would overwhelm her and she'd confess everything right then and there.

"No, I don't think so," her father said. "You could do it, but I don't think you'd want to. Charlie, do you have fifteen minutes?"

"No problem." Charlie shut off the engine and climbed out of the minivan. "What's up?"

"I'm cutting up this tree that fell in our yard during that big thunderstorm a couple of days ago, but it's taking forever. Do you think you could help me split the wood?" Mr. Cameron asked.

"No problem," Charlie said. "Let's go."

Lilly followed them to the backyard, afraid of leaving Charlie and her father alone for one minute. She sat at the picnic table and watched them split wood for about twenty minutes. When they were done, they had a large stack of logs that would be ready for the fireplace as soon as the wood dried.

"You're all set for January," Charlie told her father, picking a splinter of wood off his shirt.

"Thank you so much, Charlie. I'd have spent my whole weekend out here without your help," Lilly's father said. "Let me make it up to you. How'd you like to come over for dinner this week? Say Thursday?"

What? Her father had never invited any of Lilly's friends to dinner before. Especially not any of the guys she'd dated. And now he was inviting the boy she *wasn't* dating.

"Oh, you don't have to do that," Charlie said.

"I know, but I want to do something. Come on. We'll have fun. You and Lilly can spend some time together, and I promise I won't have any chores saved up for you."

Charlie laughed. "That's a really nice offer. But . . ." He glanced at Lilly, as if trying to gauge her reaction. "I think I'm pretty busy this week. I'm not sure I can make it."

What? Charlie was actually trying to get out of dinner with her family. How dare he! She thought he'd had as much fun that afternoon as she had.

"I'm sure Lilly would love for you to come over, Charlie. Wouldn't you, Lilly?" her father asked.

Lilly nodded. It would be fun to see Charlie again. Besides, she didn't want her father to suspect anything. "Come on, Charlie—my dad's a great cook."

"Well . . . okay," Charlie said with a shrug.

"Great! Then it's a date—or whatever you guys call them these days. See you Thursday," Mr. Cameron said.

That was when Lilly remembered she had a date with Bryan on Thursday night. They were going to study and then watch a movie at his house. She'd finally convinced him there was nothing between her and Charlie, that they were just friends—and now she had to cancel her date with Bryan to go out with Charlie. He would never believe the truth. What was she going to do? Her life was completely out of control.

"And now my dad's over at the fire station, getting his car washed to help Charlie with his fundraiser," Lilly told Tracy on Sunday afternoon. "Charlie Roark is everywhere all of a sudden."

"At least it sounds like you had fun yesterday," Tracy said.

Lilly fiddled with the bottle of nail polish on her dresser. She hadn't told Tracy everything about her afternoon—especially not about that kiss. She was afraid Tracy would tease her. Charlie wasn't like the guys Lilly usually dated. Besides, Lilly wasn't even sure that the kiss meant anything. Maybe she'd just gotten caught up in pretending to Benny that she liked Charlie. In any case, she needed to make some sense of it herself before she shared it with Tracy. "Yeah, we had an okay time," Lilly admitted.

"Maybe I got this Roark guy all wrong. He made a bad first impression, but it sounds like he's fun to hang out with," Tracy said.

"Sure, he's fun and all, but that's beside the point. I have to break my date with Bryan because

Charlie's coming here Thursday night. How am I going to explain this to Bryan?"

"Easy," Tracy said. "Lie. Bryan will never know the truth. And I'm sure he'll go out with you another night."

"I hope so," Lilly said.

"And maybe having Charlie over for dinner will turn out to be more fun than watching a movie with Bryan."

"But I don't *like* Charlie that way," Lilly protested. "And besides, I'm going to be too nervous to eat a thing with Charlie and my dad sitting at the same table. What if they start talking about cars?"

"You'll change the subject," Tracy said with a laugh. "Fast."

Chapter Eleven

LILLY JUMPED, CATCHING herself before she nodded off. She had been listening for what seemed like a very long time to a woman with very short blond hair who was babbling into the microphone.

"You're probably saying to yourselves, 'Oh, this doesn't matter, I'm sure I'll get a good job. That's so far in the future. What does it matter now?'" The blonde paused for dramatic effect. "Well, it *does* matter, people."

Lilly cringed whenever anyone called her "people," and so far this woman had done it at least a dozen times. Lilly stared mindlessly at her classmates around her in the school auditorium. They had to attend the annual spring assembly for all juniors, where they learned about all their options for the future. *As if we don't already know them,* Lilly thought. The assembly would last all afternoon, and even though it was only one-fifteen, Lilly felt as if she'd been there for hours.

Lilly glanced up at the banners hung above the stage, advertising different speakers and organizations. *Fail to Plan, Plan to Fail,* read one. *You Can Do It! Achieve Your Aims at Ames Junior College,* read another. She realized that this assembly would, in fact, be helpful: now she knew all the things she was *not* going to do with her future.

"At least we're getting out of all our afternoon classes," Tracy leaned over to say.

"Actually, I think algebra might be better than sitting through this," Lilly joked, speaking as softly as she could.

"And be thankful we're sitting within decent viewing distance of Mike Campbell," Tracy said. She stared at Mike for a minute or so, then turned back to Lilly. "Your date's all set with Bryan, right?" she whispered. "You're going out Saturday?"

"Yeah. And Paul called about Friday night. I hate having three dates in a row, so I said maybe next weekend instead," Lilly said.

"I thought you said Charlie Roark was *not* a date," Tracy reminded her, looking confused.

"Oh, I know. I just hate having plans three nights in a row." Lilly paused. "If I tell you something, do you promise not to laugh?" she whispered to Tracy.

"This sounds good. Of course I promise."

"You're not going to believe this, but when

Charlie and I went to that barbecue on Saturday, we . . . we kissed."

"You what?" Tracy blurted out, making the entire row in front of them turn around. "Mind your own business," Tracy said, then turned back toward Lilly. "You guys kissed?" she whispered.

Lilly nodded. "I know, it's crazy. And the strangest part is, I think I liked it. I mean, it started out as part of the bet, but . . . Oh, I don't know. Every time I think about it now, I get this little shiver."

"One of *those* kisses," Tracy said knowingly. "It's time to face reality, Lilly. You're falling for Charlie Roark."

"But how can I fall for Charlie? When I think about how different we are—how we hang out with different crowds, don't have any of the same friends, don't even like the same food or music or—"

"Who cares? If the guy gives you a kiss that you can't stop thinking about four days later, who *cares* about having things in common?" Tracy sighed. "I can't believe it. My best friend is finally falling in love!"

"Wait a second," Lilly whispered. "I didn't say anything about love."

"You don't have to!" Tracy said. "It's obvious."

"No way. I am not in love with Charlie Roark. He just happens to be a good kisser, that's all."

"Suit yourself," Tracy said. "But if I were you, I'd be lining up *all* my dates with Charlie. Who needs those other guys?"

Luckily, the head of the counseling department

announced a fifteen-minute break before they began part two of the assembly. "And I don't want to see any empty seats when we resume," she said. "We'll continue at one-forty-five."

"Oh, joy." Tracy stretched her arms over her head. "A fifteen-minute break."

"I think I'll get a drink of water," Lilly said. She didn't want to talk about Charlie anymore. In love? Yeah, right. Half the time she could barely stand the guy. She was just getting carried away, and so was Tracy.

Lilly made her way through the crowd and went out to the hallway. She spent at least five minutes just waiting in line at the water fountain, talking to people she knew, waving to others as they walked by.

Then she wandered back into the auditorium. As she made her way toward all her friends gathered up front by the stage, she saw Charlie and a group of guys standing off to the side. Lilly was surprised to feel her pulse beat a little faster at the sight of him. It was strange, but inside she was glad to see him.

Charlie looked cute in an oversized striped T-shirt that looked like something from the fifties. Charlie's blue eyes seemed to light up when he noticed Lilly. He didn't acknowledge her, but that was normal for them—they almost never spoke at school.

That's stupid, Lilly thought. After all, he was coming to her house for dinner. She decided to go over and say hello.

"That woman is like a cliché machine," she

heard Charlie saying as she got closer. "'People, this is Carol—listen, people.'" He imitated her voice perfectly.

"She's like someone on an infomercial," one of his friends added. "But the scary thing is that if it was really late at night, you'd be thinking of ordering the tapes right about now."

"Why don't they just get to the facts?" Charlie said. "Let's face it, half of us are going to end up working at McDonald's, and the other half—"

"Will go to college," his friend said.

"No. The other half will work at Burger King," Charlie said, and all of his friends started laughing.

"Unless they start offering veggie burgers, where are *you* going to work, Charlie?" Lilly interrupted, stepping closer to them.

"Well, if it isn't Lilly Cameron without her subjects," Charlie said. "Next year's homecoming court is standing over there, live and in person. Shouldn't you be with them?"

"And here's the Greater Middleton Deadhead Club," Lilly replied. "So glad you could all stop mellowing out and join us today."

"Touché." Charlie smiled at her. They stepped away from his group of friends, who were all staring at her as if she'd just told them Frisbees were no longer being manufactured and they'd have to hold on to the ones they had. "So, what's important enough to tear you away from your friends and talk to *me?* You're not going to bother me about a paint job for your new clunker, are you?"

"No . . ." Lilly said slowly. "And it's not going to be a clunker, if you give me that deal we talked about. Actually, the reason I came over here is—"

"You want to disinvite me to dinner tomorrow night?" Charlie asked.

"No! C'mon, stop interrupting me," Lilly said. "I just wanted to ask you—I mean, well . . . How much money did you make at the car wash? Was it successful? I would have come, only, as you probably remember, I don't have a car."

"Well, your dad was there in some car that was definitely not the Bug. Guess he wouldn't trust us with it," Charlie said. "He's a really nice guy."

"Yeah. You and my dad have a lot in common," Lilly said. "You both think you grew up in the sixties. Only my dad has a birth certificate that proves it."

"Hey, the sixties are a state of mind," Charlie said. "Ask anybody."

"Anybody *you* hang out with, you mean. So, what about the car wash?"

"It was great. We raised a little over five hundred dollars. That may sound like a lot, but that won't go too far."

"Maybe not, but it's better than doing nothing," Lilly said. "The important thing is you participated, and you did something for a cause you really believe in."

Charlie tapped his chin and stared at the ceiling. "You know, that sounds suspiciously like the motto of the pep squad."

"So what if it is?" Lilly challenged him. "I believe it's true."

"Yeah. You have a point there," Charlie said. "It does count, even if it's only a small amount."

"And if you hold it every year, or every season or whatever, it'll add up to a lot," Lilly pointed out.

"True. I never looked at it that way."

"Attention." The counselor tapped the microphone. "Attention, everyone. Please take your seats."

"Well . . . I'll see you tomorrow night, then," Lilly said awkwardly.

"Right. Seven o'clock. I might be a little late, though. I work Thursday afternoons until six-thirty, then I have to take a shower and change. But I'll be there."

"As long as you bathe before you come over, we don't care what time you show up," Lilly teased.

"Is there some kind of inspection I should be prepared for?" Charlie asked, folding his arms across his chest and smiling at her. "Are you going to check and make sure I washed behind my ears?"

Lilly felt herself blush. "I—"

"People! Take your seats!" the counselor insisted loudly. Lilly looked around quickly and noticed she and Charlie were two of the few people left standing. "See you tonight—I mean tomorrow," she whispered. Then she hurried back to her seat beside Tracy. Fortunately she had an aisle seat, so she didn't have to disrupt a whole row to sit down.

"How did it go?" Tracy asked in a whisper as

the counselor introduced a new speaker.

"We were just . . . talking, that's all," Lilly said.

"I could see that!" Tracy said. "But did you make any plans for the weekend? Did you tell him how you felt, how you can't stop thinking about—"

"Give it a rest, okay? Charlie and I are just friends."

"Whatever you say, Lilly," Tracy said, giving her a skeptical look.

Charlie felt like a fool. He was standing outside the Camerons' front door, carrying a small box of cookies his mother had insisted he bring.

"Hi." Charlie looked up as Lilly opened the front door. "What's that?" she asked, staring at the box in his hands.

"Oh, these are for you, for your family." Charlie handed the cookies to her.

"Thanks. Um, come on in." Lilly stepped aside and made room for Charlie to walk through the door into the kitchen. "Charlie, this is my mother, Bridget Cameron."

"Hi, Charlie. It's nice to meet you. Help yourself to some iced tea," Lilly's mother told Charlie.

"Excellent. Thanks." Charlie poured himself a glass from the pitcher on the kitchen table.

"Don't worry, Charlie, I already warned my mom about your eating habits," Lilly said.

"Actually, your coming over gave me a chance to try a new vegetarian stir-fry recipe," Mr. Cameron said. "How's it going, Charlie?" He turned from the wok where he was cooking and waved with a spatula.

"Fine, thanks, Mr. Cameron," Charlie said.

"Call me Curtis. Dinner will be ready in about ten minutes. You guys have plenty of time to hang out by yourselves."

"Look, Charlie brought us some cookies," Lilly said. "Wasn't that nice?"

"I'll put them on a plate," Mrs. Cameron said. "Thanks, Charlie."

"Oh, no problem. My mother made them," he said, feeling incredibly awkward. He was wearing a white shirt and his best baggy black jeans, and he was actually wearing *socks* with his sneakers.

"So . . . this is your house," Charlie said, looking around at all the knickknacks and prints on the walls as they moved from the kitchen into the living room. He smiled when he saw the family pictures on the mantelpiece next to a bunch of cheerleading trophies.

"You've been here before," Lilly said. "Remember? The day you brought the car back," she whispered.

"Right. I remember," Charlie said. It seemed like ages ago. He remembered how Lilly had almost knocked him over to get a look at the car, and how they'd had nothing to talk about. Things were a lot different now. Charlie almost felt relaxed with her around.

"Here's something you'd probably die for. Something my dad will never part with." Lilly

123

pointed to a poster on the wall behind the couch advertising a Grateful Dead concert back in the 1970s.

Charlie moved closer to get a better look. The poster was amazing. "Tell me something. How does your dad feel about theft?"

"Well, I think he likes you, but I wouldn't push my luck if I were you. Let's just say he feels almost as strongly about this poster as he does about his car."

Charlie nodded. "Okay, then. Let's move on. Hey, how about showing me your room?" He looked around for the stairs.

"Okay, but first you have to promise you won't make fun of everything in it," Lilly said.

"I won't," Charlie promised. "Not that you haven't made fun of everything I like and believe in."

"Yeah, but there's a difference—I'm always right."

"Oh, yeah? You really think so?" Charlie grinned as he took a step closer to her.

"Yes, that's exactly what I think." Lilly looked up at him, nodding. "Of course, it *is* hard being right, and perfect, all the time."

"Don't I know it," he joked, leaning his hand against the wall beside her. He looked at Lilly's face, trying to measure her expression. She seemed really happy to see him, almost as glad as he felt to have a chance to spend some more time with her. Time that had nothing to do with the bet. Then again, she might just be putting on a show because of Sweetpea and her father. *Just ask her,* Charlie told himself. *Find out if she likes you as much as you like her.*

"Dinner is served!"

"Guess that means us," Charlie said nervously, taking a step backward.

Lilly's face was flushed pink. "Guess so."

Charlie followed Lilly into the dining room, where everyone sat down—Mr. and Mrs. Cameron at each end of the table, and he and Lilly facing each other across the table. Lilly's father served large helpings of the stir-fry on rice and passed them around the table.

"Charlie, I've been trying to get an answer out of Lilly for hours now, and I'm hoping you can help," Mrs. Cameron said, picking up her chopsticks. "How did you two meet?"

"Oh, uh, at school, Mom," Lilly said. "I mean, where else would we meet?" She dumped several squirts of soy sauce onto her food and gave Charlie a conspiratorial grin.

"Yeah, we have English class together," he added. "But we didn't really get to know each other until recently—" He paused as Lilly shot him a panicked look. "—when Lilly wrote a story for the paper on that car wash last weekend. Thanks for coming, by the way."

"Glad to help." Lilly's father took a sip of iced tea. "So, Charlie, what do you do to keep busy? Lilly's told us absolutely nothing about you, as usual."

As usual? Charlie thought. Was Lilly constantly having boys over for dinner with her parents? Was this just some familiar routine for her? He'd never had dinner at a girl's house—a girl who was more than just a friend.

"Well, my job is what keeps me busiest. I haven't had much time for anything else recently," Charlie said.

"Really? Where do you work?" Mrs. Cameron asked.

"Dad, the carrots in this stir-fry are fantastic," Lilly blurted out. "Really crispy, and they have a kind of ginger taste. Is there ginger in this?"

"Yes. Thanks for the compliment." He looked at Charlie expectantly. "So where do you work?"

"Roark's Auto Body," Charlie said. "My dad and uncle own it."

"I've seen that garage," Mr. Cameron said. "Fortunately, I haven't had to come in for service yet."

Not that you know about, anyway, Charlie thought as Lilly handed him the pitcher of iced tea.

"Then you know a lot about auto-body work?"

"Um . . . I know some." Charlie nodded. "They're training me. Not that I want to do that forever, but I kind of enjoy it."

"What would you rather do?" Mrs. Cameron asked.

"Well, I'm really into alternative fuel sources. I'd like to work on developing some of them or promoting them for companies that provide them. Like the improvements they've made in electric-powered cars and stuff like that."

"Really." Mr. Cameron looked at Charlie and

nodded. "That's a great ambition. I believe we all need to help our natural world, instead of hurting it the way we have been."

If only my father was as understanding as Mr. Cameron, Charlie thought. His father wanted him to take over the business when he turned thirty. He'd told his father he'd consider it only if they repaired electric or wind-powered cars.

"In fact, I've thought about trying one of those electric cars myself, but we have two cars and I just can't give one of them up. I have a 1968 Volkswagen Bug," Mr. Cameron said.

"Really?" Charlie tried to look surprised. "That's a great car." Lilly nudged his shin under the table with her foot. "I mean, I've always wanted one of those, they look so cool. I've never driven one, though." He reached over and squeezed Lilly's knee. A small smile curled the corner of Lilly's mouth.

"Maybe we can go out for a spin one day," Mr. Cameron said. "Although it's been running a little rough lately. I think I need to bring it in to my mechanic for a tune-up."

Lilly dropped her fork onto her plate. As Charlie watched her forehead crease he wished he could tell her not to worry. A mechanic wouldn't find anything wrong.

"It's probably nothing," Charlie told her father. "I wouldn't worry." He smiled at Lilly. Her secret was safe with him.

Chapter Twelve

"REMEMBER WHEN YOUR dad was telling that funny story about getting a tattoo for a concert he went to?" Charlie asked when he and Lilly went outside to his car after dinner. "And how your mother's parents were horrified?"

Lilly groaned. "I've heard that story *so* many times. It's, like, his favorite story to tell my friends."

"Well, I have a tattoo," Charlie confessed.

"No way! Really? Of what?"

Charlie nodded. "A bear. You'd probably hate it. I didn't say anything at dinner because I thought your parents might not like it, like maybe it was fine for your dad, but not for me. But I guess it doesn't really matter what they think of me."

"No, I guess not," Lilly said. "Actually, my dad would just think you're cooler than he already does, if that's possible." She stopped beside an old, weather-beaten station wagon. "Are you ever going to show up in the same car twice? I feel like I'm dating a used-car salesman," Lilly said. Then she felt her face turn bright red. She was glad it was pitch black outside. "I guess that's kind of a moot point now, since you won't be showing up here anymore."

And we're not dating, really. We never have been. Lilly felt a little confused about what exactly had gone on between them. Was it all a show, or was some of it real? Now that the bet was over, would they ever see each other socially again?

"So, I'll see you at school," Charlie said. "Same old same old."

"Yeah."

"Well . . . take care." Charlie got into his car and started the engine.

"Sure. You too," Lilly said. "Don't eat too many bean sprouts."

She watched as the station wagon's taillights went down the block and disappeared around the corner. So that was it. Charlie Roark was out of her life. That was what she wanted, what she'd been waiting for ever since their first date.

Then why do I feel so let down? she wondered. Lilly was about to walk into the house when the station wagon came back down the block, Charlie honking the horn. "Hey, Lilly!" he called, slowly coming to a stop.

"Did you forget something?" Lilly asked.

"Yeah. I forgot I owe you a hot-fudge sundae. Feel like heading to Sandy's with me?"

Lilly grinned. "I'd love to—let me grab my coat!"

"When you came back to get me tonight, I couldn't help thinking about how you took off in the tow truck that day in the rain," Lilly said to Charlie as they sat in a booth at Sandy's ten minutes later.

"And you were about as happy to see me coming back tonight as you were then, right?" he joked, digging his spoon into a tall sundae dish of mint chocolate chip ice cream and hot fudge.

"No. Actually, both times I was *thrilled*. First you got me out of a major disaster with my parents, and then tonight you saved me from doing the dishes. You've got great timing." She took a sip of water as she looked at Charlie.

"Really? I always thought you'd rather do anything than hang out with me."

"At first we didn't know each other," Lilly said. "But after the grueling social events we've been through, I think we can handle anything."

"Even a large group of your friends?" Charlie pointed toward the door with his spoon.

The gang Lilly usually hung out with was walking into Sandy's: Kelly, Tracy, some guys from the football team, some guys from the soccer team, and Bryan Bassani!

Lilly slowly wiped her mouth with a napkin and wished the floor would open up and swallow her alive. She wasn't embarrassed to be seen with Charlie; she just couldn't understand why Bryan always bumped into them whenever they went out together. Bryan was definitely going to think Lilly and Charlie had something serious going on between them now and would think she was off limits. She'd never get to know Bryan at this rate.

She tossed her napkin down on the table. "Let me just say hi real quick, then I'll be back."

"No problem," Charlie said, standing up. "I'll come with you."

Lilly didn't know what to do. She and Charlie had been having a great time, and she couldn't just tell him to get lost. But how could she explain that right now his timing wasn't good—it was awful! She walked over to Tracy and Kelly, all too aware of the fact that Charlie was beside her, and Bryan, her date for Saturday night, was watching her every move.

"Hey, guys, what's up? You all know Charlie, right?" Lilly said.

Charlie nodded at everyone as they said hello to him. "How's the catering going?" he asked Bryan.

Do you have to remind him that he saw us there together? Lilly wanted to scream, shooting Tracy a panicked look.

"Okay," Bryan said.

"I'd die if I had to wear that uniform. That ruffled shirt— it's like something my mother would wear."

Bryan glared at him. "Well, it beats wearing coveralls and crawling underneath cars," he said in a snide voice.

"You think so?" Charlie replied.

"So anyway, what are you up to tonight?" Lilly

asked Kelly, trying to change the subject. She didn't want Charlie and Bryan to talk or argue with each other. Her life was difficult enough at the moment.

"Do you have a problem with me working for a garage? What's the matter, isn't it good enough for you?"

"It's fine," Bryan said with a shrug. "If you like being a grease monkey. Personally, I'd rather—"

"Carry serving trays around and offer sushi to guests?" Charlie interrupted. "Yeah, that's challenging, all right."

"Guys, guys," Lilly said nervously. Why did Charlie have to insult Bryan? And what was Bryan's problem, anyway?

"Lilly, I think our ice cream's melting," Charlie said, turning to her. "Want to go back to our table?"

"Actually, I want to talk to my friends," Lilly told him. What right did he have to try to drag her away? Just because he and Bryan didn't get along?

"Lilly, what time should I pick you up on Saturday? Does six sound okay?" Bryan asked.

Charlie glowered at him.

"Six would be good. I'll be right back, okay?" She tugged Charlie's sleeve, half dragging him across the restaurant to their booth. "What is *with* you?" she demanded.

"I just don't like that guy," Charlie admitted.

"Well, I *do*," Lilly said. "And I'd appreciate it if you didn't walk around insulting my friends!"

"He was rude to me too," Charlie grumbled.

Lilly threw up her hands. "What are you, twelve years old? Can't you just try to get along with people who are different from you?"

"Not when they're snobby and rude, no."

"Bryan's not like that."

"Yeah, right." Charlie shook his head. "Why don't you just try and see people for what they really are?"

"I see a big, judgmental jerk in front of me right now!" Lilly said. She grabbed her jean jacket from the booth. "I'll get a ride home with my friends, thanks."

"Lilly, wait. I didn't mean to be a—"

"Too late, okay?" Lilly said. "Look, it's been fun, but let's just call this a done deal. Your bet is over and we don't have to see each other anymore." She turned, walked across Sandy's, and took a seat beside Bryan in the booth. A few seconds later, she saw Charlie leave.

Halfway through lunch period on Friday, Charlie spotted Lilly in the cafeteria. He felt bad about the way he'd acted the night before—though was it his fault he'd gotten jealous when he saw how excited Lilly was to see that Bryan guy?—and he wanted to apologize. He hated leaving things on such a bad note. He'd thought there was something special between them, a connection that didn't have anything to do with the bet. *Obviously you were wrong, buddy. Big-time wrong.*

He screwed up all his courage and walked toward Lilly's table. And she got up and began walking toward him. *Great—we're on the same wavelength!* he thought excitedly. Charlie smiled at Lilly as she came closer. "Hey, Lilly."

"Hi, Charlie. How's it going?" she asked.

"Pretty good. Listen, I have something really funny to tell you. You're not going to believe this."

"That's great, but I can't talk right now."

"It'll only take a second," Charlie said. "First, I just wanted to say—"

"Charlie, I don't *have* a second," Lilly replied, sounding irritated. "I have to get up to the student council office and check on some information about the prom." She walked right past him, out the door, and into the hall.

Charlie just stood there in the middle of the cafeteria for a second, people passing by on either side of him. Lilly had given him the ultimate cold shoulder. Here he was, ready to confide his feelings for her, and she was busy thinking about decorations for the prom.

The prom. Charlie made a face. *I wouldn't be caught dead at any school-sponsored dance that includes decorating the gym and crowning people like they're royalty.* Lilly was probably planning to go with Bryan. Well, he hoped they'd have a great time standing around thinking about how much better they were than everyone else.

My first impressions of Lilly were right, he

thought. *She's a superficial, shallow human being.*

And it was obvious that she'd meant what she'd said the night before. She wanted Charlie out of her life—for good.

Chapter Thirteen

LILLY LOOKED AS if she'd been standing in front of a large fan for two hours—in the rain. Staring in the restroom mirror at Sandy's, she took a brush out of her pocketbook and tried to get rid of some of the tangles in her hair. Bryan had taken her to Sandy's in his new white convertible, which was nice . . . only it was windy, and drizzling just enough to get her wet, and her hair had turned into a sticky mess.

I can't believe I looked like this all through dinner. I look almost as bad as I did the afternoon of the accident, she thought. *When I met Charlie.*

This was her first Saturday without seeing Charlie in three weeks. First the accident, then the wedding, and then the barbecue. She'd only seen Charlie briefly Friday, and that was more than enough. She still couldn't get over how rude he'd been Thursday night.

Now she was finally out with Bryan Bassani, whom she'd had her eye on for at least a month. Only so far, the mystery wasn't turning out to be very intriguing at all.

Maybe I just don't know him well enough yet, Lilly told herself. She took a last glance at herself in the mirror before going back out to their booth.

"Ready to roll?" Bryan asked when she returned to their table. He wiped his hands on a napkin.

"Sure," Lilly said. "But the movie doesn't start for another half hour."

"I know, but I like to get there early and get a good seat," Bryan said.

"Okay, whatever," Lilly said with a shrug, leaving a tip on the table. On their way outside, she waved to Kelly and Jake and some other people she knew at different tables. She almost wished she and Bryan were staying at Sandy's with everyone else, instead of going off to the movie.

"You know a lot of people," Bryan commented as they got into the convertible. "That's cool."

"Yeah," Lilly said. She tried to think of something else to say, but nothing came to mind.

Bryan started the car and slowly pulled out of the parking lot. She was glad he'd finally put the top up when they arrived at Sandy's; now at least she wasn't getting wet. She tapped her foot against the floor in time to a song she liked on the radio.

"This is a great song to dance to," she said to Bryan as he braked for a stoplight.

"I don't dance," Bryan said matter-of-factly.

"Oh." An image of a smiling Charlie moving around the dance floor flashed through her mind. "Why not?"

"I just don't like to," Bryan said.

Lilly nodded. That was a good enough reason, she guessed. She stared out the window as Bryan took a right turn going about five miles an hour. They were going so slowly, it would be a miracle if they even made it to the Cineplex in half an hour. She felt as if she were driving with her grandmother.

Maybe he's going so slow because it's such a new car and he doesn't want to take any chances. Lilly thought of Charlie, barreling around corners in the tow truck. She wondered if he'd be so cautious with a new car. Weren't you supposed to have *fun* in a sporty car? Wasn't that the point?

"What kind of music do you like?" she asked Bryan, trying to make conversation. "Since you don't like to dance, I guess it wouldn't be dance stuff."

"I like all kinds of music. It doesn't really matter to me."

Lilly turned to him. "It doesn't? Aren't there some bands you love, and some bands you just can't stand?"

Bryan shrugged and put on the turn signal. "Not really."

So you have no opinions at all? Lilly wanted to ask. *About anything?* So far the only thing that Bryan had seemed passionate about was that his hamburger be cooked medium-rare—not rare, he'd told the waitress, and not medium.

"Honey, I've been working here for ten years. I know what medium-rare means, and so does the cook," she had told him, and Lilly had laughed.

Only Bryan hadn't. He didn't have much of a sense of humor, especially not when it came to himself.

How could I have talked to him so many times and never noticed this about him? Lilly wondered as they pulled into the Cineplex parking lot. Bryan drove around for about ten minutes, searching for the perfect spot close to the door. When they finally got out, they had only five minutes before the movie was supposed to begin. They hustled to the ticket window.

"Two for *Murphy's Law*," Bryan said.

"Wait a second. Wait, don't give us the tickets yet," Lilly said to the woman behind the ticket window. "I thought we were seeing *Blue Monday*," Lilly said to Bryan.

"We were, but I read this review in the paper today that said *Murphy's Law* is supposed to be great. Lots of chase scenes and special effects."

And we all know how much I love those! Lilly thought. How could he just choose the movie without asking her? "But *Blue Monday*'s supposed to be good, too," she argued. "You know, kind of weird and funny."

"Today, please? There are people waiting behind you," the woman behind the window prompted.

"I still say *Murphy's Law*," Bryan said.

Lilly shook her head. "Whatever. I mean, that's fine."

Murphy's Law, she thought. *Doesn't that say that whatever can go wrong, will?*

The woman behind the window gave Lilly a sympathetic look and punched out the two tickets.

They entered the crowded theater and Lilly looked around for people she knew. And suddenly she noticed the one person she was trying to avoid: Charlie Roark. He was standing on line with a group of his friends at the snack counter.

"I think I'll get some jawbreakers," Bryan said. "Want anything?"

"No, thanks." Lilly stood in line, waiting for Charlie to turn around and notice her. She thought about saying hello first, but knew Charlie would only give her a hard time about being out with Bryan. She decided to stay put and wait to see if Charlie noticed her. If he saw her, she'd pretend she hadn't seen him and say a friendly hello.

But Charlie didn't turn around. His friends got some popcorn—he got a cup of water, of course—and they headed over to the usher who was tearing tickets in half. "Four for *Blue Monday*," he announced. "Second door on the right."

That figures, she thought. *Charlie's going to the movie I wanted to see. If I were on a date with him . . .*

Bryan turned toward her, a giant box of jawbreakers in his hand. "Let's go, or we'll miss the previews," he said nervously.

"It's not my fault we're late!" she said, annoyed.

Bryan looked at her. "I didn't say it was."

Lilly pointed at the box of candy as they walked underneath the glowing sign that said *Murphy's Law.* "You know, those things are murder on your teeth. I don't know how you can eat them."

"I like them," Bryan said, looking confused.

Lilly slumped down into her seat beside him as the lights dimmed. *He doesn't even know how to argue well!*

The only mysterious thing about Bryan was why she'd ever thought he was interesting in the first place. She'd never been on a duller date in her life.

If only I were here with Charlie instead, she thought. *We'd see a great movie, laugh at the same things . . . I'd actually be having fun right now.*

Lilly realized she missed Charlie. A lot.

Maybe Tracy was right. Maybe I am falling in love with Charlie Roark, she thought. *Then why am I on a date with somebody else?*

Monday afternoon Charlie had just opened his locker when he saw Lilly hurrying down the hall toward him. For a second he felt a rush of excitement at the thought that she was hurrying because she wanted to catch him before he left. Then he remembered that she had cheerleading practice and the gym was at the end of the hall, just past his locker.

He wondered if she'd seen him at the Cineplex on Saturday night. It hadn't taken her long to bounce back into the social swing, Charlie thought. She was back to her three-dates-a-week schedule, no doubt. Meanwhile, Charlie was hanging out with his pals, as usual. There was nothing wrong with that. He'd just gotten used to hanging out with Lilly, that was all.

And you'll just get un-used to it, he warned himself. It wasn't as if they'd spent massive amounts of time together.

"Hi, Charlie!" Lilly said.

"Hi, Lilly." Charlie leaned back against his locker. "So, how did you like the movie the other night?"

"You did see me," Lilly said, shifting her blue gym bag to her other shoulder. "Why didn't you say anything?"

"Why didn't *you?*" he replied, hooking one of his sneakers on the bottom edge of his locker and resting his books on his knee.

"Well, by the time we got through the snack line, you guys had already gone into the movie," Lilly said. "What's your excuse?"

"I saw you and Bryan having a little disagreement by the ticket window," he said. "And I didn't want to get in the middle of anything. But you were right—you should have gone to see *Blue Monday*. It was great."

"*Murphy's Law* was horrible. It was like a bad cop drama on TV stretched out to two hours instead of one. So predictable. Someone either got into a car chase or got shot every ten minutes, min-imum," Lilly said, shaking her head.

Charlie laughed. "Sounds like your kind of flick, all right."

"Yeah. Anyway, I'm glad I ran into you, because I've been wanting to ask you something."

Charlie's eyebrows shot up. "Really?" The last time he'd talked to Lilly, she didn't want anything to do with him.

"This is going to sound really stupid," Lilly began, scuffing the floor with her sneaker. "But I miss you, Charlie."

"Really?" Charlie asked. "Are you serious?"

Lilly nodded. "Hard to believe, but true."

"No! I mean, I was just standing here thinking the same thing," Charlie admitted. "But I figured you were busy dating other guys and you didn't want me hanging around."

"That's what I thought," Lilly said. "I couldn't wait to get back to my life, but you know what? My life's boring. Without you around, nobody makes fun of me or argues with me. It's totally dull."

Charlie grinned. "Really?"

"Can't you say anything else except 'Really'?"

"Like what?"

"Like, how about if we go out tonight?" Lilly said. "I don't know what we can do around here on a Monday night that's fun, especially since I have to be home at eight to study, but—"

"I have an idea," Charlie said. "How about if I pick you up around six?"

"What are we going to do? Where are we going? What should I wear?" Lilly asked.

"Just trust me," Charlie said, "and dress casual."

Lilly glanced up at the clock on the wall. "I have to run or I'll be late for practice. I'll see you tonight!" She jogged off down the hall toward the gym, her long hair in a neat ponytail, her gym bag slung over her shoulder.

I have a date with Lilly—a real date! Charlie had to restrain himself from jumping up and down. *Lilly said she missed me!* Charlie was so excited, he felt like following Lilly to cheerleading practice, turning cartwheels.

It's official now. I've completely lost my mind.

"This is one of your favorite places in town?" Lilly asked Charlie, looking around the Maine Lanes, a bowling alley she'd driven past a hundred times without once going in. She and Charlie each picked up a pair of bowling shoes at the counter and headed over to their assigned lane.

"Want anything from the snack bar?" Charlie asked, lacing up his red-and-blue shoes.

"No, thanks. This is so cool, Charlie. I think I was eight years old the last time I went bowling." She finished tying her shoes and picked up a green bowling ball. "Green was always my lucky color. Wait, don't tell me—you brought me here because you're a great bowler, and you're going to humiliate me, right?"

"No, of course not. I just like hanging out here

because I can be alone. No one from school ever comes here."

Lilly smiled. If Charlie thought getting the two of them alone in a bowling alley was a private, romantic date, then he was even more offbeat than she'd thought. But after half an hour, when they'd bowled a game, laughed a lot, and congratulated each other, she was having so much fun that she started to think Charlie was right—this was the perfect place for a date.

Other guys with no imagination would take me to Lovers' Lane, not the Maine Lanes, she thought, watching Charlie twist his body to the right as the ball he'd just rolled down the lane veered into the left gutter.

"That's my third gutter ball in a row," Charlie complained, sitting beside Lilly at the scorer's table. "What's happening to me?"

Lilly turned to him and shrugged. "You're falling apart, Charlie. Another gutter ball and you might as well retire from the world of bowling for good."

"I *am* good. I don't know why tonight I'm playing as if I'd never bowled before."

"I wonder why. Could it be that you're intimidated by my immense power?" She curled her arm, flexing her bicep.

Charlie wrapped his hand around her arm. "No, but it could be that I can't stop looking at you. You look so cute in those bowling shoes and you're so pretty, even under these horrible fluorescent lights."

Lilly smiled, and Charlie put his hand on her cheek.

"Why did we always fight before?" she asked softly.

Charlie leaned over and kissed her once, then twice, then caught her up in a kiss that was so sweet and wonderful, it seemed to last for hours.

"Charlie," she began when they finally broke apart, "I have a question for you."

"Go ahead," Charlie said, twirling a strand of her hair around his finger.

"I know you think school events are dumb, but would you consider going to the spring formal with me?"

"You mean the prom? Aren't you going with that soccer dude?"

"No! Definitely not. I'd much rather go with you."

"I hate school dances. They're so lame," Charlie said. "But the way I feel right now, you could ask me to slide down that bowling lane over there on my stomach and knock all the pins over with my body and I'd do it. You could ask me to do anything, and the answer to everything would be yes."

Lilly smiled. *I'm going to the prom with Charlie!* "So, do you think you can hit one of those pins or what?"

"Lilly, I've just hit all ten!"

Chapter Fourteen

WHAT A GREAT time! Lilly thought as she got ready to take a shower, change into her pajamas, and start her homework. She'd had as much fun with Charlie as she'd wished she'd had on her awful date with Bryan on Saturday night. *How could I have thought Bryan was the one? I was so wrong—Charlie's the guy for me.* She whistled along to the radio, reaching into her closet for her robe.

"Lilly?" There was a loud knock at the door. "Can you come downstairs, please? We want to talk to you about something," her mother said.

"Oh. Okay." Lilly shrugged. She quickly put on her robe and hurried downstairs to find both her mother and father in the kitchen. Her mother was at the table and her father was pacing back and forth in front of the dishwasher.

"What is it?" she asked. Seeing the distressed looks on both their faces, she was starting to get worried. "Is it Grandma?"

"No, it's not Grandma," Mr. Cameron said angrily.

"Curtis, take it easy," her mother said.

"How can I take it easy?" He shook his head. "Lilly, I need to ask you something, and I want you to be honest with me. Completely honest. Like I hope you always are."

Lilly gulped and sat down on the stairs. "Sure. Go ahead." This didn't sound good. She had never seen her father so upset.

"Have you ever used Sweetpea without our permission?" Mr. Cameron asked.

Lilly couldn't even open her mouth. She didn't know what to say, so she just nodded.

"You have?" her mother asked, genuinely surprised.

That made Lilly feel even more terrible. They trusted her so much . . . and she'd really let them down. "Yes," she said. "Only once."

"But once was long enough to get into an accident, wasn't it?" her father prodded. "And you never told us you used the car, or that you wrecked it, or that anything happened."

"I—I didn't know how to tell you," Lilly admitted. "I was afraid you wouldn't let me drive again, and that you'd never let me have my own car—"

"Well, you're right about that." Mr. Cameron tapped a spoon against the counter. "You are one hundred percent correct there. We won't be letting you use the car or have your own car, Lilly. I don't even want you to *look* at my car. In fact, maybe we should hold onto your driver's license just to make sure you don't use it, since obviously our asking you *not* to doesn't have any effect."

"Curtis, there's no need to—"

"Yes, there is!" Lilly's father stared at Lilly, and she looked down at the floor. "Tell me how it happened."

Lilly took a deep breath. She was shaking all over, and she knew she was going to start crying any minute. She hated getting into arguments with her parents. She hated when they were angry with her, especially when she knew they were right. "It was the weekend you went away, a few weeks ago," she choked out.

"I knew it!" Mr. Cameron slapped his palm against the counter. "We go out of town for one lousy weekend—"

"Let her finish," Mrs. Cameron urged. "Go on, Lilly."

"I only went out for a little bit," Lilly said, sniffling. "I had to . . ." She thought about lying, saying she'd had to get some groceries, then realized lying would only make things worse. As if they could possibly get worse. "I had to get something at the mall."

"The mall?"

"You guys don't understand! I know it sounds terrible, but I was going *crazy* that day. It was raining so hard—I just had to get out of the house," Lilly explained. "I know that's no excuse for what I

149

did; I'm just telling you what happened. I was only going about five miles an hour when I ran into a stop sign. The bumper got kind of messed up—"

"I'll say," Mr. Cameron said. "And if you go out to the garage now, you'll see that it's *still* messed up. It's barely attached to the car."

"So that's how you found out."

"Yes, and I don't appreciate not being told what's going on with my own car. Do I have to remind you that it's a classic automobile?" Lilly's father asked. "And you ran into a stop sign on the way home from the *mall?* Lilly, I can't believe this! How could you lie to us?"

"I . . ." Lilly began, but she realized she had nothing to say. She knew that she'd panicked and made the wrong choices. Besides, Charlie had fixed the car—at least he'd *said* he had.

Only Charlie hadn't fixed the car at all! He'd done some halfhearted job, all so he could get a date with her and win that stupid bet with his cousin, not caring what would happen to her when the car fell apart. How could he do that to her? *I should have known better than to trust a laid-back, tuned-out total drag of a sixties wannabe to fix a car right!* she thought angrily.

"Well? What do you have to say, Lilly?" Mrs. Cameron asked. "How could you do such a thing?"

"I just . . . made some bad decisions. Really bad decisions," she added when her father glared at her. "I'm so sorry, and I'll pay for the garage to fix the car again."

"So you *had* it fixed?" her father asked. "Where? Some cut-rate garage? At a convenience store?"

"No. Roark's Auto Body," Lilly said.

"Isn't that Charlie's father's—" her mother began.

"So that's how you met." Her father scowled at her. "How convenient. Wreck my car, get a new boyfriend."

"He's not my *boy*friend, and I didn't plan anything, Dad! I'm sorry!" Lilly cried, a tear rolling down her cheek. "What else can I say?"

"We have a few things to say," Mrs. Cameron said. "We trusted you and you let us down. Now I'm afraid we need to make sure this doesn't happen again."

Lilly stared at a crumb of bread on the floor and wiped her eyes. She knew what was coming, and it wasn't good news.

"First, we'll deduct the cost of the repairs from your summer earnings. And second, we're going to have to ground you, for at least a month. After a month, we'll see," Mrs. Cameron said.

"A *month?*" Lilly saw her whole life turning into a dull routine: school, home, school, home . . . How was she supposed to keep up with everyone and everything at school when she had to stay home every night? And what about the prom? she wondered—would she have to miss that too? Not that she even wanted to go with Charlie anymore, now that he'd messed up her entire life. She didn't want to see him again—ever! He'd betrayed her in the worst way possible. It might have all been some elaborate game to him, but this was her life, and now it was ruined.

Mrs. Cameron got up from the table and walked over to Lilly. "Look, why don't you go upstairs for a little while? Your father needs to calm down," she said in a soft voice. "We'll talk more later."

"Mom, are you guys ever going to forgive me?" Lilly asked, wiping her wet cheek with the sleeve of her robe.

"In a while, I'm sure," her mother said. "But for now, we need to let your father's temper cool down."

Lilly nodded and stood up. "I'm really sorry," she said. Then she turned and walked up the stairs. She had just reached the top when she heard the phone ring.

She started walking back down the stairs but paused on the landing halfway down when she heard her father's voice. "Lilly can't come to the phone, Charlie. I'd rather not go into it with you right now, if you don't mind. Suffice it to say that she can't talk to you now or anytime soon. Good night." Then Lilly heard her father hang up the phone with a bang.

She ran into her bedroom and threw herself on the bed. It was all painfully obvious to her now: she'd been a fool to believe Charlie liked her, to believe that his dating her had ever been anything more than a way for him to win a bet. She'd traded her feelings for some dumb car repair that he hadn't even cared enough about to do right!

"Thanks a lot for blowing me off last night. I just called to tell you what a terrific time I had with you, but if you didn't want to talk to me, you could have told me yourself. You didn't have to have your dad get rid of me."

Lilly's face was bright red when she turned around from her locker to face Charlie. He hoped she was good and embarrassed for the rotten way she'd treated him.

"Well? Are you going to apologize?" Charlie asked her as a few people passed by them in the hall.

"Apologize? Charlie, that's so ridiculous it's almost funny. Only I'm not laughing, because I have some serious problems at home, all thanks to you!" Lilly exclaimed.

"Thanks to *me?*" Charlie asked, confused. "What are you talking about?"

"You didn't really fix my father's car at all, that's what I'm talking about," Lilly said, stepping closer to him. "The bumper fell off on one side and started dragging along the road as my dad was driving home from work yesterday!"

"What?" Charlie stared at her.

"Good thing you don't plan on going into your father's business, because as far as I can see, you're totally incompetent."

"I am not," Charlie argued. "Look, I'm sure I can fix whatever it is. I'll tow it right after school and have my dad look at it."

"Wrong again," Lilly said. "My father brought

the car somewhere else this morning. I guess he figured he'd rather have someone who's not a tattooed hippie wannabe fix his car this time. Call him crazy."

"You're the one who's crazy," Charlie said. "This isn't my fault at all. If you hadn't gone off to the mall in his vintage car in the first place, you wouldn't have had to lie to your dad and make a deal with me to get it fixed overnight."

"I wish I'd just told him the truth," Lilly continued, "instead of making some stupid deal with you, Charlie. I know you wanted to go out with me just to win a dumb bet. Well, congratulations. You're the lucky winner. But don't expect me to be happy for you, not after the way you used me."

"What are you talking about?" Charlie asked.

"Last night. The kisses. You and me. Us. It was all part of the bet, wasn't it? You and Benny haven't figured out who'll go on that cruise, so you decided to see just how much you could get out of me!" Lilly said.

"No, that's not it at all! That wasn't part of the bet. We're going to settle it with a poker game. Benny's a terrible poker player and—"

"Give it a rest," Lilly said. "I don't believe anything you say anymore. This bet has always been about getting a date with me, and then getting another date. But that wasn't enough for you. Now you've obviously decided you need to make me fall for you so you can hurt me, too."

"Lilly, I never intended to hurt you," Charlie

said. "I care about you. A lot. I mean, I think I love—"

"Look, Charlie, just leave me alone," Lilly said, her voice quivering. She took a book out of her locker and slammed the door closed. "And tell Benny to have fun in Alaska. Congratulations. You won. But don't ever talk to me again!" She walked down the hall, and Charlie followed her. Then she started running. The first bell rang, and she disappeared into the crowd of students heading for homeroom.

Charlie wandered upstairs, barely aware of the crush of students around him. He vaguely heard people saying hello to him, but he was too dazed to respond. He couldn't make sense of what had just happened. Lilly, the girl he was crazy about, the girl who'd made him feel things he'd never felt for anyone before, the girl he was in love with, had just told him to get lost for good. She didn't trust him, she didn't believe him. She didn't want to see him ever again.

He felt as if the bottom of the world had just dropped out from underneath him. And he had no idea what to do next.

Chapter Fifteen

"SO CHARLIE'S A jerk, just like we thought in the first place. He did some lame repair work, got dates with you—and now his dumb repair isn't even any good," Tracy said Tuesday afternoon during lunch in the cafeteria. "And he had the nerve to do it all for some bet. Unbelievable." She broke off a piece of her peanut-butter cookie and offered half to Lilly.

"No, thanks. I'm not hungry." Lilly was busy tearing the napkin on her tray into tiny shreds. "I'm so mad I can't even eat."

"Don't think about it," Tracy advised. "Don't think about *him*."

Lilly let her gaze wander around the cafeteria. She didn't see Charlie anywhere, and she was glad. Not that it would help her stop thinking about him. All during English class she'd had to stare at her notebook to avoid looking over at him as she used to do, and she'd bombed a quiz in French class thinking about him.

Charlie probably aced that quiz, she thought now. *There was nothing to get in the way of his concentration.* And that was because he didn't have any feelings. If he had, then their dates and their kisses would have meant something to him—something real. They wouldn't have been part of a dumb bet that had been going on for almost a month now. What he hadn't considered was that she wasn't just part of a bet—she was a real, live, breathing girl with feelings. Feelings that didn't deserve to be trampled on. Feelings that she didn't understand or even like having. *I liked kissing Charlie,* she kept thinking. *A lot.*

She and Charlie weren't meant to be together. They didn't *belong* together. And they couldn't agree on anything for more than two minutes, tops. But something had happened between them— love, maybe?—or so she'd thought.

Tracy finished eating the cookie and took a sip of cranberry juice. "I probably don't need to tell you this, but there are easily a dozen guys I can think of who would treat you better than that, Lilly. You deserve a lot better than Charlie the creep."

Lilly shrugged, making a pile out of the napkin pieces.

"We should have trusted our instincts from the very beginning," Tracy said. "We never liked Charlie—not until he grew on you."

157

"Yeah. He seemed like a decent, honest guy. We really had fun together. . . ."

"But he turned out to be just some scammer who got you into trouble with your parents. And if that's not bad enough—ooh." Tracy shuddered. "I get so angry thinking about it, I just want to find him and punch him."

Lilly gave a small sigh. "Now that would be worth watching."

"I know—we can make it an event, kind of a sideshow at the prom. Holden versus Roark, the ultimate showdown." Tracy spoke in a deep, announcerlike voice. "Coming soon to pay-per-view."

Lilly smiled. She was glad she had Tracy to cheer her up. For a couple of minutes she forgot about Charlie, about how bad she felt, and about how angry she was.

"Come on, let's go up to the *Herald* office before lunch is over and see what's happening," Tracy said. "That'll get your mind off Charlie." She picked up her brown paper lunch bag and stuffed her trash into it.

I doubt it, Lilly thought as she picked up her tray and brought it over to the dishwasher. *Maybe if I just keep busy and get back to my own life, the way it was before I met Charlie, I can pretend this whole, humiliating situation never happened.*

But she couldn't get her mind off one question: How could Charlie have kissed her so intensely if it didn't mean anything to him?

She couldn't forget his eyes, his laugh, the way he danced, and how it felt to hold him close. . . . Didn't he have *any* feelings for her?

"What's *he* doing here?" Tracy pointed toward a booth in the back of Sandy's.

Lilly craned her neck to get a better look. Charlie.

"He never comes here," Tracy added. "Well, except for the other night, when he was here with Lilly."

"Maybe he's trying to turn over a new life—I mean, leaf," Kelly said.

"Good one!" Tracy said, laughing. "Turn over a new life. Yeah, he could use one. And a new personality too."

Lilly looked at Kelly and shrugged, pretending she didn't care one way or the other who Charlie was, or whether he was there. Nobody besides Tracy knew about what had happened between her and Charlie. And there was no point in telling anyone, especially now that it was all over, Lilly thought.

It had been two days since their fight. Lilly couldn't help wondering if Charlie had come to Sandy's hoping to run into her. And if he had, he sure wasn't going to approach her while she was sitting in a booth with five of her closest friends. Maybe he wanted to apologize.

She decided to give him a chance. But she wouldn't walk over to his table—that would be going too far. No, he had to come to her. That would tell her whether he was really there to see her or not. "Does anyone need anything?" she asked the group. "I'm going to get some more ketchup."

"I have some packets here," Kelly volunteered.

"You'll probably want those," Lilly said. "Be right back." She strolled over to the counter where all the condiments, napkins, and silverware were. She slowly drew a packet of ketchup out of a bin, and then another.

"Hey," Charlie said, suddenly appearing behind her. He had come up while she was trying to avoid looking in his direction. "What's up?"

Lilly just turned around and looked at him, waiting.

He bit his lip. "So. What's happening in the world of the blond and popular?"

"I wouldn't know," Lilly said, "seeing as how I'm not blond."

"Right." Charlie laughed nervously. "Hey, I'm having lunch with Aunt Margaret Sunday. Wish me luck. I'll be sure to mention that you've started your own collection of post–World War I dollhouse furniture. I'm sure she'll be very impressed."

Lilly sighed loudly. "Charlie, is there a *point* here? Because I'd really like to get back to my friends."

"Actually . . . there is something I have to tell you." Charlie's expression changed slightly.

Good. We're finally getting down to something serious, she thought. *It's about time.*

160

"I'm seriously thinking about ordering a cheeseburger here, and I need you to talk me out of it," Charlie said.

Lilly shook her head and looked over at the door, completely exasperated. "Charlie, for one thing, I don't care what you eat, and I never have. And for another, when you're really ready to talk to me, give me a call or something. But don't stand there making jokes and expect me to laugh after what you did to me."

"What I did to you?" Charlie asked, looking confused. "Lilly, I only wanted—"

"You only stomped all over me, is what you did. It was a big game for you and Benny, but it was my life. Now, thanks to you, it's a crummy life, but at least you're out of it. So if you'll excuse me, I have to hurry home, because I've been grounded for a month. See you later."

Lilly stormed back to her table, head held high even though she felt as if she was crumbling inside. She grabbed her book bag from the booth seat.

"Leaving so soon?" Tracy asked. "Wait a second—you're not leaving with *him,* are you?" she whispered.

Lilly shook her head, not trusting her voice.

"Oh, right—the old four-thirty curfew," Tracy said. "I'll call you tonight, okay?"

"Bye, Lilly!" her other friends called out.

Lilly managed a muffled "Bye!" and waved to everyone, then hurried outside. She was glad to see Charlie's battered old station wagon pulling out of the parking lot. She hid for a second by the door, not wanting him to see her.

Then, when he was gone, she turned and walked toward home, though she didn't make it a block before she burst out crying.

She'd never felt so terrible and mixed up in her life. And it was all because of Charlie Roark, someone she hadn't even known a few weeks earlier. Now, a month later, her whole life had been turned upside down.

"I have a pair of aces," Charlie said. "What about you?"

"Three of a kind." Benny grinned. "Read 'em and weep." He fanned his cards out on the table, then pulled the pile of red and white poker chips toward him.

"Whatever," Charlie said.

"You are losing bad, man." Benny pointed at the small stack of chips left in front of Charlie. "What's the deal? You always beat me."

Charlie slid a red chip back and forth on the table in Benny's living room. Benny was right; Charlie had won every game of poker they'd ever played together. Benny had no poker face whatsoever—if he had a good hand, he smiled; a bad hand and he scowled. Charlie had almost felt guilty taking money from him in the past, only they'd played for such small stakes it hadn't really mattered.

That night it wasn't small stakes, though. They were playing to decide, once and for all, who was going to Alaska with Aunt Margaret. And Charlie didn't even care if he went or stayed home, or that he was wasting his Saturday night sitting there with Benny when he could have been out with his friends at the coffeehouse.

All he could think about was Lilly. *What's the deal?* he wondered as he looked at the cards in his hand. *I've never felt so . . .* He couldn't describe how he felt, not even to himself. All he knew was that it felt like going into a skid on a patch of ice. Out of control.

He had another lousy hand, but he matched Benny's bet. The sooner he ran out of chips, the sooner this whole thing would be over. "Two, please." Charlie traded in a two and a six. Benny gave him two cards: a three and a five. Charlie tried to laugh. He'd never seen such lousy cards in his life.

Benny laid down his hand. "Full house, can you believe it?"

"No, I can't." Charlie tossed his cards onto the table and put his head in his hands. "Can't we just flip a coin and end my misery?"

"C'mon, we're almost done," Benny said. "Dude, I hate to break it to you, but you're going to Alaska."

"I can see that," Charlie said. "Look, let's just call it a night, okay? You win, I concede."

"What's your rush?" Benny asked. "Got a date you haven't told me about? Hey, whatever happened to Lilly, anyway? I thought for a while there that you guys were hitting it off."

"So did I," Charlie said with a sigh.

"So? What's the problem?"

"You are," Charlie said. "And I am. It's all about that stupid bet we made. She thinks I'm only interested in her to try to win."

"That's stupid," Benny said. "Didn't you tell her we were playing poker tonight to decide who would go?"

Charlie nodded. "Yeah, but she wouldn't listen."

"No way. She's really mad at you, huh?"

Charlie thought about the look on Lilly's face the day they'd fought, and how irritated she'd seemed when he approached her at Sandy's. He'd wanted to tell her how he really felt about her. That the bet had nothing to do with them, nothing to do with how she made him feel, especially when they kissed. But instead he'd made some dumb joke about the food. He'd been so nervous, he couldn't do anything *but* joke. And he'd blown it, big time.

"Yeah, she's mad all right," Charlie told Benny, who was methodically counting his chips. "She didn't believe me when I said we were playing poker to decide."

"Maybe she'd believe *me*," Benny suggested. "I'll call her for you. She has to listen to me."

"She does?" Charlie asked. "Since when?"

"Look, Lilly and I got to be pals, kind of. She'll take my word for it."

Charlie shrugged. "It's worth a shot." He couldn't imagine Lilly believing Benny, but he was desperate. Maybe if both he and Benny were saying the same thing, Lilly would forgive him. "Okay, let's call her. You talk first, okay? If she hears it's me, she might hang up."

"No problem. I'll convince her. Then you'll talk to her, and everything will be cool." Benny picked up the telephone on the coffee table. "What's her number?"

Charlie gave him the number and paced back and forth while Benny waited for someone to answer. "Hello. May I speak with Lilly, please?" Benny asked politely. "Oh . . . she's not home? Okay. No . . . uh, no message. Thanks." He hung up the phone and shrugged. "She's not home," he said to Charlie.

"But . . . she's grounded. She has to be home." Charlie tapped the deck of cards against the table. Was she out on another date already? Hanging out at Sandy's with her friends while he sat there feeling lousy? "Why would she tell me she's grounded and then not be home?" he wondered out loud.

"She could have gone somewhere with her dad," Benny said. "Or maybe she was taking a shower or something. Don't let it get you down. We can try again tomorrow. In the meantime, you need to start thinking about one thing and one thing only—packing." Benny laughed, and Charlie flopped onto the couch, face down.

"I'm going on a cruise to Alaska with Aunt Margaret," he muttered. "What a total drag." Then he got an idea—a way to ease his conscience. If he couldn't settle things with Lilly, at least he could try to make things up with her parents.

★   ★   ★

"You just missed Charlie," Mrs. Cameron said when Lilly got back from jogging later that evening.

"What?" Lilly panted, wiping her forehead with the sleeve of her T-shirt. She'd just run a five-mile loop around the neighborhood. She loved it when Daylight Savings Time started and she could go running in the evening when it was still light.

"He came by to talk to us," Mr. Cameron said.

"Oh." Lilly tried not to sound too disappointed, but she couldn't help herself. Why hadn't he stopped by to see *her?*

"Hey, what's with that T-shirt? I've never seen you wear it before," her father said.

Lilly looked down at the T-shirt her father had given her after the Grateful Dead concert he'd gone to a few years before.

"You're not doing this just to make up with me, are you?" her father asked.

"No," Lilly said.

"Well, it's working anyway." He smiled at her. "A few more weeks and we'll be okay."

Lilly smiled back and sat down in the chair opposite the couch. At least her father was talking to her again. He'd barely said a word to her all week. "I figured I'd better try something to make you less mad at me," she said.

"I have a funny feeling Charlie helped change your tune. He may not be able to fix cars very well, but he does have good taste in music. Actually, he's quite a responsible young man. He apologized for the work he'd done on the car and offered to pay for the new repair. He's got a lot going for him."

Lilly hesitated for a minute. She'd never talked to her parents about boys before. But then, there had never really been anyone to talk about.

"Actually, Charlie and I . . . well, we're through, you know," Lilly said. "I mean, we barely even got started, and then it was over."

Her mother looked at her, her expression full of sympathy. "That's too bad. What do you mean, barely got started?"

"It's just . . . I don't know," Lilly began. "I thought I hated him. Then I started to like him. He's not like any guy I've gone out with before. I thought things were good between us, and maybe he was the person I was supposed to be with, and then—well, he acted like a real jerk, Mom. I mean, what he did, it's huge. Hugely bad."

"Oh." Her father looked uncomfortable. "You're not mad at him about what happened with the car, are you? You can't hold him responsible for your mistake."

"I don't," Lilly said. "Maybe at first . . . but not now. It's not about that."

"What's it about, then?" her father asked.

Lilly shook her head. "It's too complicated." *And too painful,* she thought. "I'm going upstairs to take a shower." She stood up.

"Lilly? Have you tried talking to Charlie?" Mrs. Cameron asked. "Maybe that would help."

"I tried," Lilly admitted. "He turned it into a joke."

"Give him another chance," her mother urged. "Maybe he wasn't ready last time."

"Maybe." Lilly turned and went upstairs, where she turned on the radio, flipping the dial until she landed on the classic rock station.

"Next up, a classic set from one of our favorites here at WMDL—Crosby, Stills, and Nash," the disc jockey said.

That's a sign, Lilly thought. *I bet Charlie's listening to this right now. He probably even requested it.*

She skimmed the list of phone numbers she had tacked to her bulletin board. She had scrawled Charlie's number down when he was fixing the car and had told her to call if she needed to know something. "Hello, is Charlie there?" she asked when a woman answered the phone.

"No, I'm sorry, he's not," a friendly woman—probably Charlie's mother—replied. "He's over at his cousin's. Can I take a message?"

"Yeah. Tell him . . ." *Tell him he just missed out,* Lilly thought. "Oh, never mind. Forget it. Thanks." Lilly hung up the phone and grabbed her robe from the back of the closet door.

She didn't want to hear the songs on the radio. She didn't want to hear anything that reminded her of Charlie. Her heart was broken in two, and it was all his fault.

Chapter Sixteen

"HEY, DID YOU go out with Paul last night?" Tracy asked Lilly on Sunday morning when she called.

"I'm grounded, remember? Anyway, I've decided I don't want to go out with just anybody," Lilly said.

"You know what my mother always says. You have to kiss a lot of frogs—"

"To find a prince," Lilly finished. She pictured a frog with Charlie's face. "Maybe so, but right now I don't feel like dating just to date. I'm still trying to deal with what happened between me and Charlie. I know you don't know what I mean, but—"

"No, I understand. You really liked Charlie, even though he might have acted like a jerk. I think you're still in love with him."

"Tracy, you think everyone's in love," Lilly said. "You're always saying that."

"Maybe. But you've never said these things about any other guy you've dated. Like about how your days are empty now, or how much you miss him. Lilly, when most guys ask you out, you're not even that excited."

"Sure I am," Lilly protested. "Maybe I just don't show it."

"And maybe they're just not the right guys," Tracy said. "But Charlie is. Oh, I can't believe I said that. Mr. I'm-too-groovy-for-this-school, too-groovy-to-be-cool—"

"He doesn't think that," Lilly interrupted, laughing.

"There you go defending him again. Look, if you're going to spend the whole day pining, at least let me come over and pine with you," Tracy said. "There has to something we can do together that's better than sitting around feeling rotten. I know what will cheer you up. Let's go to the mall. I want some pizza, and you want to look at . . . what do you want to look at?"

Lilly had to think for only a second. "Sneakers. I want a new pair of sneakers." Not purple, but maybe some blue ones. Or maybe the ones with two colors. She didn't really care—as long as they were just like Charlie's.

"And here's the cabin we'll be sharing." Aunt Margaret handed Charlie a thick brochure, open to a page in the middle.

"Sh-sharing?"

"Of course, that's not the exact one. The ship has several hundred rooms. That's just an example." Aunt Margaret dabbed at the corner of her mouth with a napkin. "What do you think?"

Charlie looked around the restaurant where they were having lunch. "I thought we'd have separate rooms," he said.

"Oh, no," Aunt Margaret said. "This will be fun."

"But . . . isn't it going to be a little cramped?" Charlie pushed his fork around his empty salad plate.

"We're family," Aunt Margaret said. "Don't you want to stay together?"

"Sure. Whatever," Charlie said. He'd rather sleep on the deck than share a room with Aunt Margaret, but it wasn't worth arguing about now. He had about six weeks to get used to the idea. Or, if he looked at it another way, six weeks to get out of going. *Maybe I'll come down with mono.*

"Charlie, are you feeling all right?" Aunt Margaret asked, adjusting the bright yellow and pink scarf around her neck.

Charlie cleared his throat. "I might be coming down with something. I don't know."

"You don't seem sick, just sort of blue. Now you know me, I hate to pry, but I haven't heard anything about that pretty Lilly in at least a week," his aunt said, ignoring his attempt to start building his illness defense. "Oh, I completely forgot to give this to you. Here, I got double prints of that picture I took at the wedding of the two of you." Aunt Margaret reached into her large purse and pulled out an envelope of photographs. She searched through them and then handed two pictures across the table to Charlie.

Charlie glanced at the photograph. In it, he and Lilly were standing underneath a tree, his arm around her shoulders, and they were about to kiss—their first kiss. She was smiling. And it didn't seem like a forced smile, as if she'd been out with him only because she owed him. She'd looked so beautiful that day.

"You'll give one to her, won't you?" Aunt Margaret asked.

"Oh, sure," Charlie said. "As soon as I see her."

"Everything all right between you two?"

"Actually . . . no," Charlie said. "She thinks— well, she thinks I don't really care about her. But I do, Aunt Margaret. More than you can imagine."

"I can see that. So what are you going to do about it?"

"Do? I don't know," Charlie said. "I've got to do something, though. I'm miserable without her."

Aunt Margaret studied his face for a moment. "You really love this girl, don't you? Come on, you can tell me anything, you know that."

Charlie nodded. "Yeah, I guess I do love her."

"Maybe you can answer a question for me, then. How does Lilly feel about traveling?"

"I don't know. Why?" Charlie asked, puzzled.

"Well, I might be able to help you out here. Do you think she'd like to come with us on our cruise?"

"What? You wouldn't mind if Lilly came with us?" Charlie almost fell out of his chair.

"I'd love to have her along," Aunt Margaret said. "She's perfectly charming. And the two of you could have a lot of fun together. Just picture how romantic it'd be—oh, it'd be like a movie, wouldn't it? Of course, I'd be chaperoning the two of you very carefully." She gave Charlie a stern look.

"Oh, of course." Charlie nodded. "So is it okay if I go invite her? Do you really mean it?"

"Charlie, I always mean what I say," Aunt Margaret said. "Have you ever known me to back out on a promise? Find Lilly. Invite her—see if that helps you make up with her. Then call me and give me all the details!"

Charlie jumped up from his seat. "Can I borrow this brochure? I want to show it to Lilly."

"Certainly. Be my guest."

"Thanks a lot, Aunt Margaret."

"Oh, I haven't done a thing," she replied. "Shoo, shoo. Go find Lilly and I'll phone her parents. We'll get this straightened out in no time." She winked at Charlie, and he leaned over and kissed her cheek.

"You're the best, Aunt M.," he told her before he ran out of the restaurant at top speed, almost knocking over a busboy who was carrying a full tray of glasses.

"Mind if I put my feet up?" Lilly asked Tracy.

"Go ahead. My car is your car." She turned up the

radio, and Lilly propped her feet on the dashboard.

Lilly thought about when she'd first met Charlie and he'd offered her a ride home. She remembered how she'd dreaded sitting next to him. He'd said he wouldn't want to torture her, and then he'd driven away. Now the torture was not being able to sit in his truck, the truck she'd complained about so often. She wouldn't be anywhere near him ever again.

She'd have to forget about Charlie and move on.

Still, she hoped there was some way they could work things out. They had known each other for only a short while. Maybe they just needed more time. But Lilly knew summer was coming, and that was when they'd drift apart. Everyone did their own thing in summer. Then senior year would begin and they'd be further apart than ever.

"Are you thinking glum thoughts again?" Tracy asked. "You've got a look on your face that says the world's about to end. Now quit it. There's no need to lose hope."

"That's easy for you to say. Isn't this light ever going to change?" Lilly said impatiently.

The car in front of them inched forward. Tracy took her foot off the brake and moved ahead behind it. But the light was still red. "They need to fix the timing on this thing," Tracy said. "This is ridiculous. Nobody is even coming the other way."

"I know," Lilly said, looking around. "Oh, there it goes. *Finally*."

They'd just begun to move ahead when their car was bumped from behind—not too hard, but hard enough to move them forward. Lilly braced herself, quickly putting her hands on the dashboard. "What was *that?*" she asked.

"We've been rear-ended! I can't believe it!" Tracy exclaimed. She whipped off her seatbelt and stormed out of the car.

Lilly slowly got out after her. This was the second accident she'd been involved in over the past month. She felt like a car jinx. She put her hand over her eyes to shield them from the sun.

The door swung open on the car behind theirs. It looked an awful lot like Charlie's old station wagon, the one with the front fender mashed in.

"Oh, no." Tracy shook her head. "It can't be."

"It can and it is," Lilly said, her heart beating faster.

Chapter Seventeen

CHARLIE GOT OUT of the car, his hands shaking. He looked at Tracy, then at Lilly, and felt as if he was going to faint. The combination of seeing Lilly sooner than he'd expected and having just bumped into someone else's car was too much for him to handle. Meanwhile, the drivers behind them were honking and gawking at the three of them.

"Hi," he said quietly.

"Hi?" Tracy practically shouted. "*Hi?* Is that all you're going to say?"

"Uh . . . I guess I wasn't paying attention," Charlie said, suddenly thinking of his father. Whenever people brought smashed cars into the shop his dad would always point to the driver's handbook. There was a section in it that said people shouldn't drive if they were sad, upset, or angry.

"Emotions can have a marked effect on your driving," he'd always say.

I shouldn't have been driving, Charlie told himself. He'd been so busy thinking about what he was going to say to Lilly when he got to her house that he hadn't even seen the stoplight, even though he must have been through this intersection a hundred thousand times before.

"So you're not a perfect driver," Lilly said. "Gee, I'm shocked."

"Well, actually, you guys should have—"

"Don't even try to make this my fault." Tracy's arms were folded across her chest as she glared at him. "Just get ready to call your insurance company, because my mother's *not* going to like this." She walked around, inspecting the damage to the back of the car. One of the taillights was broken, but that seemed to be all that was wrong. "Nice," she said. "I can't believe this."

"I'm sorry," Charlie said meekly. "It's all my fault. You're right." Out of the corner of his eye he saw Lilly smiling. Then she started to laugh. "What's so funny?" he asked.

"You are. You must have told me ten times what a bad driver I was. At least I didn't bump into someone else's car!"

"Stop sign. Same thing," Charlie said.

"Yeah, but I didn't claim to be world's most perfect driver. You did," Lilly said, laughing even harder.

Tracy walked over to him. "At least Lilly isn't

going to use this to get a couple of dates from *you*. Not that she'd want to date you. Then again, maybe she would. You'd better talk to her."

"What?" Charlie asked, twisting the cruise brochure in his hands.

"Do we have to file an accident report or what?" Tracy asked. "I can't remember."

"It depends," Charlie said. "Only if there's a certain amount of damage to the vehicle, and I don't think this is enough. Definitely not enough to call the police."

"What's the matter, are you nervous?" Lilly asked, walking over to him. "Are you afraid of what your parents are going to say when they find out what happened? Gee, imagine how that must feel. I can hardly picture it."

"I'm going to call my mom and see what I should do." Tracy pointed to a pay phone across the street. "I'll be back in a few minutes."

"It's not even raining today," Lilly said. She pointed at the bright sun. "Perfect driving weather. Do you mean it's still possible to get into an accident when you're an excellent driver and the weather's fine?"

Charlie sighed, exasperated. "Look, I get it, okay? Stop rubbing it in. Anyway, it's your fault I got into this accident in the first place."

"And just how do you figure *that?*" Lilly asked.

"Because I was on my way over to your house to show you this." He shoved the brochure at Lilly. "This tells you all about the cruise we'll be taking."

"We?" Lilly asked. "You and me?"

Charlie nodded. "I lost to Benny playing poker last night. And you can call him or Aunt Margaret or anyone you want if you still don't believe I went out with you because I liked you and not for any other reason!"

Lilly moved closer toward him and took the brochure from him. She started leafing through it. "This looks nice," she said. "But what do you mean, *we're* going on it?"

"I just had lunch with Aunt Margaret. And when I told her how upset I was about losing you, she suggested I invite you along. She's going to call your parents, and if they say it's okay, we'll set sail sometime in early June," Charlie said, his heart pounding.

"Are you *serious?* Am I really going on a cruise with you?" Lilly said excitedly, grabbing Charlie's arm. "But wait. I think I'm still mad at you."

"What for? I mean, come on, Lilly—what else do I have to do? Stand on my head? I never wanted to hurt you. It's like I tried to tell you that day in school—I love you."

Lilly threw her arms around Charlie's shoulders and hugged him tightly. "And I love you! Even if we do make the weirdest couple I've ever seen."

"Weird is good. I can deal with that." Charlie smoothed a lock of her hair back behind her ear. Lilly looked into his eyes. Then he leaned forward and kissed her gently. "Can you believe we're going to Alaska together?"

179

"No," Lilly said, "I can't. But I think it's the best thing that's ever happened to me."

"Besides wrecking Sweetpea, of course." Charlie pulled Lilly even closer to him.

"That's definitely the high point of my life," Lilly agreed. "If I hadn't, I never would have gotten to know you. I wouldn't be standing here now, kissing you in the middle of an intersection. And Charlie, I can't imagine not being here with you. I'm crazy about you. I want to be with you all the time."

"The same goes for me," Charlie said, kissing her again.

There was a loud honk from a car, and Lilly and Charlie turned around. Tracy had come back from the phone, and she was reaching into her car, honking the horn repeatedly, waving and smiling at them. "Way to go, Lilly and Charlie! Another victory for true love!"

"Don't mind her," Lilly said, taking Charlie's hand as they walked over to Tracy.

"I won't." Charlie squeezed her hand. "From now on, the only person I'm going to pay any attention to is *you*."

"Finally we agree on something," Lilly teased, and Charlie put his arms around her waist. He had Lilly back, and life was perfect!

Except for the fact that he'd just wrecked his parents' station wagon.

Do you ever wonder about falling in love? About members of the opposite sex? Do you need a little friendly advice but have no one to turn to? Well, that's where we come in . . . Jenny and Jake. Send us those questions you're dying to ask, and we'll give you the straight scoop on life and love in the nineties.

DEAR JAKE

Q: *I like this guy—let's call him Billy—and I think he likes me too. We have tons of fun whenever we hang out together—alone. But when Billy's with his friends, he totally ignores me. He's like Dr. Jekyll and Mr. Hyde, and I just can't take it, Jake. What's Billy's problem?*

DB, San Juan, PR

A: For most guys, it's difficult enough to approach a girl he's interested in when there's no one around, so imagine how hard it would be to do it in front of his *friends.* Billy might be afraid of being rejected, so he may have decided that it's safer to ignore you (especially if he's shy). Or he might think his friends will tease him if he shows any interest in you. Approach Billy the next time he's alone and strike up a conversation. Let him know you're interested in him, and hopefully that will boost his confidence enough that he'll feel less awkward running into you when he's with his friends. If he still seems shy, act friendly, but don't be too pushy—you might scare him off. Eventually, if he does like you, he'll definitely show you in his own way.

Q: *A few weeks ago I met a nice (and really cute) guy named Sean. We hit it off right away, and before we knew it, we were kissing like crazy. I was so excited. Finally, the love of my life! But yesterday a nosy girl named Veronica pulled me aside at lunch and informed me of Sean's extracurricular activities. It seems he's still seeing his ex-girlfriend, who'd moved to another town just before we'd started dating. I don't want to believe Veronica, but if she's right, how can I continue to date Sean? Please help. . . .*

SB, Beaumont, TX

A: Okay, this won't be easy, but you've got to get up the courage to face Sean and ask him, straight out, if he's still seeing his ex-girlfriend. If Veronica's right, it's better to find out directly from Sean. If it's true, then you've got to make a difficult decision. Should you leave him fast, before you become even more attached to him, or stick with a no-win situation? Whatever you do don't take Veronica's word for the truth until you confront Sean. If you break things off with Sean without talking to him first, you run the risk of losing a guy who may truly love you and *only* you.

DEAR JENNY

Q: *For the past few months, all my best friend, Ann, has done is talk about her major crush on Evan—a guy in our class. She's afraid to approach him alone, so she always begs me to go* *along with her (for moral support) when she gets up the nerve to talk to him. Now for my problem . . . as a result of hanging with Ann and Evan, I've developed a crush on him myself. And I think Evan's begun to feel things for me too. How am I going to get myself out of this mess? I want what's best for my friend, but what's best for me is worst for Ann!*

GC, Gary, IN

A: Whew! I've been through this myself, and believe me, it's no picnic. You need to decide who's more important to you—your best friend or this guy. Have you been friends with Ann for years? Built a lifetime of memories? Well, if so, is the possibility of dating Evan worth losing something so strong? If you go ahead with plans to date Evan, be prepared to lose your friendship with Ann. And then you'll have to deal with your guilty conscience. Talk about painful. Regardless of your decision, you must be honest with Ann, and you must be honest with yourself. While you may hurt Ann at first, it will be much better in the long run if you tell her about your feelings for Evan yourself, rather than have her find out about the two of you the hard way—through the grapevine.

Q: *Last summer I began dating a twenty-one-year-old guy named Rob. I was a hundred miles away from home, and fifteen years old. Now that I'm home, I'm dying to visit Rob—but my parents refuse to give me permission! They think I'm too young to be involved with a guy in his twenties. They think he's bad news—but they've never even met him. I know they want me to* *date guys my own age, but fifteen-year-old guys are so immature—especially now that I've dated Rob. How can I convince my parents to let me see him? He's so important to me. Help!*

BG, Sag Harbor, NY

A: Convincing your parents will not only be difficult, it may not be worth the effort. Why hasn't Rob ever come to visit you? He's obviously old enough to drive—or take a bus if he doesn't have a car. If he's truly interested in continuing your relationship, he should be willing to compromise. Have him meet your parents, and together you can tell them how much you mean to one another, that they should treat you like the young adult you are. Explain why they should give Rob a chance. And if Rob isn't willing to do this small thing for you, then maybe he's not as "mature" as you think he is. Remember, maturity doesn't necessarily come with age. Just because he's older, doesn't mean he's more responsible.

Do you have questions about love? Write to:

Jenny Burgess or Jake Korman
c/o Daniel Weiss Associates
33 West 17th Street
New York, NY 10011